Boy Lost in Wild

Boy Lost in Wild

stories by
Brenda Hasiuk

TURNSTONE PRESS

Boy Lost in Wild
copyright © Brenda Hasiuk 2014

Turnstone Press
Artspace Building
206-100 Arthur Street
Winnipeg, MB
R3B 1H3 Canada
www.TurnstonePress.com

MIX
Paper from responsible sources
FSC® C016245

All rights reserved. No part of this book may be reproduced or transmitted in any form or by any means—graphic, electronic or mechanical—without the prior written permission of the publisher. Any request to photocopy any part of this book shall be directed in writing to Access Copyright, Toronto.

Turnstone Press gratefully acknowledges the assistance of the Canada Council for the Arts, the Manitoba Arts Council, the Government of Canada through the Canada Book Fund, and the Province of Manitoba through the Book Publishing Tax Credit and the Book Publisher Marketing Assistance Program.

The stories in this collection are a work of fiction. Names, characters, places and incidents are either the product of the author's imagination or are used fictitiously, and any resemblance to actual persons living or dead, events or locales, is entirely coincidental.

Printed and bound in Canada by Friesens for Turnstone Press.

Library and Archives Canada Cataloguing in Publication

Hasiuk, Brenda, 1968-, author

    Boy lost in wild : stories / by Brenda Hasiuk.

ISBN 978-0-88801-497-9 (pbk.)

    I. Title.

PS8615.A776B68 2014   C813'.6   C2014-905788-1

*For my parents, Ernie and Pat,
and my kids, Katya and Sebastian,*

and all those who grow up roaming Winnipeg's back lanes.

Contents

Boy Lost in Wild / 3

Back Lane Lullaby / 15

Life on Ice / 29

Blood / 47

Roma Raj / 65

Sandwich Artists / 81

Little Emperor / 103

It's Me, Tatia / 125

Boy Lost in Wild

Boy Lost in Wild

Four Facts and a Very Short Legend

1. Black bears can reach bursts of speed of 50 km/hr and can outrun a person going up- or downhill.
2. Most young black bears are forced into less preferred habitat by older, dominant bears, leaving them more likely to wander into human campsites, yards, and garbage dumps.
3. The name Manitoba is believed to come from the words "manitowapow" (Cree) or "manito bau" (Ojibway), which mean "straight of the spirit" and refer to an island in Lake Manitoba Narrows where a "manitou" or "great spirit" beats his drums.
4. Many Aboriginal families in Manitoba split their time between their home communities or First Nations "reserves" and larger cities like Winnipeg and Saskatoon.

Swampy Cree Legend

Long ago the land we know as Canada was empty. People lived in another land, up above. A voice asked a man and a woman if they would like to go to another land down below. They agreed and went to see Spider to get there. They did not heed his warnings, however, that only one person may look down from the spider's line and, when both looked, they fell into the great eagle-nest. They were rescued by a wolverine and a bear. The bear taught the pair the ways of life on this new land. This is why the bear is respected and considered a wise person. When the White-Men came, they were interested in the Indians' coats and skins, but the two groups of people did not understand each other.

It runs across the street, moving with a kind of lope. Out from behind the house that has a faded Santa waving from the roof all year long, it just appears, teetering a little from right to left, like its back haunches are too wide for its body.

Campbell watches it cross the street and disappear into the lane behind the string of long, low buildings where he works. Its coat is black and silky, almost purple in the ten o'clock dusk. Some people might think it's a dog, a Lab maybe, but there is no mistaking the lope. That lope is as familiar to Campbell as his own hands.

Seeing it here, though, in the city, is ridiculous. All he can do is stand staring at the street, now empty except for a few parked cars.

On the sidewalk, two little girls are stomping pop cans flat with their bare feet. One of them seems to be crying because it hurts.

Before he can stop himself, Campbell shouts, "Did you see that?"

The girl who isn't crying picks up a bag from the ground and holds it against her chest like a teddy bear. "These are our cans," she says.

Campbell shakes his head and walks toward them, swinging

his arms at his sides. Though the sun is almost down now, it's still hot, and the tiny breeze under his armpits feels good.

"I don't want your fucking cans," he says.

The one still cradling the bag pulls up the crying one, bawling even worse now, and pulls her away.

Campbell starts running toward them, then stops dead and waves his hands in the air like a scary monster. He shouts: "I don't want your fucking cans!"

He knows it's mean. His legs tremble as if he's just finished a long race. As the crying one gets dragged away, she gives him the finger, and Campbell doesn't even laugh. He stands unmoving for maybe a minute, feeling shaky, and then turns his back on the girls and starts walking home, through the vacant lot with the big, graffiti-covered sign that says "Great Development Opportunity," through the sour-smelling back lanes, rental yards filled with busted toys from the dollar store, old-people yards filled with big vegetable gardens and yappy little dogs, past the one with the cucumber plants bigger than him and the plywood bench that looks like a coffin.

This time, though, this hot August night, he doesn't really see anything around him and almost walks straight into a truck backing into the lane. When he gets home, and his mom passes him in the doorway and asks if he's seen his younger brother, it's like he does not hear her, and does not care.

So. The young black bear runs across the street, and disappears into the dusk. Over and over in his mind for more than two weeks. Sometimes he remembers the little girls, stomping their cans, and sometimes he doesn't. Sometimes he even remembers the cool breeze under his armpits. Other things float in from nowhere, like the orange of the sun disappearing so fast, and the half-moon still so faint that you almost miss it. But the bear is always there, plain as day, loping along, and then gone. Even now, in the ballroom of the Fairmont Hotel, the purplish black shape is moving somewhere in the corner of his eye.

Campbell knows the people at the table think he's not eating lunch because he's nervous. Most of them, who are probably a lot older than his mom, shook his hand when they sat down, and asked him questions like what grade he was in. He found that if he answered with a smile and one word, they smiled back and went on talking to each other. But Debbie, the young one who has brought him here to this room full of people in suits and feels most responsible for his success or failure, can't stop. "Don't worry, Cam," she keeps saying. "They'll heat it up for you later. It's natural to have the butterflies. Don't worry."

He nods and smiles. He knows she thinks she is helping, but the only thing that seems to soothe him right now is the loud, thick noise of five hundred people talking and cutting and eating at the same time. It reminds him of the story about the kid from up north, where he comes from, who wandered off into the boggy forest while hunting with his dad. The newspaper said searchers thought the kid probably couldn't hear their calls because the mosquitoes, millions of them, kept up a loud, relentless buzz. Maybe they'll call his name, Campbell thinks, and he will not hear. They'll have to go on to someone else, and then it will be over.

Suddenly feeling the need to move, he puts his hands on the white tablecloth. The sleeves of his borrowed suit are too long, and all he can see is his fingertips. He puts them back in his lap and stares at his plate of chicken. The mushroom sauce has cooled into a disgusting jelly. Back home, wild mushrooms grow like grass, and Campbell has never gotten used to the store-bought kind. They smell good, but have no taste.

"Really, Cam," Debbie says, "we've practised and you know it practically by heart." She keeps brushing her hair behind her ear, over and over, like a cat licking itself. "I'll make sure they don't clear away your chocolate mousse either. You don't want to miss that, believe me."

She's eaten everything on her plate except the chicken.

Campbell nods some more. He has liked her since the first time she showed up, in a yellow dress with no sleeves, and said to him, "Your supervisor says you have a big mouth, and that's exactly what we're looking for." She always seemed to throw him off his game, though. Now, he can feel his lips stretching across his teeth, like his smile is going to rip his face open. Part of him wants to reach over, punch her in the mouth, make her shut up, stop calling him Cam.

His whole body shakes a little, like he's just come in from the cold. He knows she has seen this, and this makes him want to punch her even more. Sitting right there, he can still feel the cool breeze under his armpits, even though, in this giant, air-conditioned room, his palms are sweating. Why didn't he follow it, he wonders, for perhaps the zillionth time. It couldn't have disappeared. A bear runs into the lane behind The Freak House, and goes where?

In his head, it's always "The Freak," which is what his older brothers call the place where he works. Really, it's a youth drop-in centre known as The Freight House because that's what it was when the railway was still important. His older brothers said only little faggots hung out at The Freak, so Campbell stopped telling them where he went, until he got a job there. After that, his brothers still called him a little faggot when they borrowed money, but with a smile, as if they didn't really mean it.

"Cam," Debbie whispers across the table. "Do you see the agenda?"

Campbell notices the room is quieter now, and the lights are dimming. Under his water glass, a little soggy, is a piece of paper with fancy printing. He left it there on purpose, because when he first sat down and saw his name, he thought he might throw up on the white tablecloth.

"First the Minister of Family Services, then the Mayor, then you," Debbie says, holding up her agenda and pointing. She does this in the special way she has of making him feel stupid without meaning to. When he sees her hands are shaking, though, he fights the urge to reach over and touch them in the dimness, to feel how smooth and hard her pink nails must be.

"We're saving the best for last," she says.

The room is now completely dark, except for a bright light at the front. On a small stage covered in yellow flowers in pots, a guy in a suit introduces another guy in a suit. Campbell sits very still and tries to follow. But their words are only sounds in his head: *a hand up instead of a handout; empowering the disenfranchised to make good choices; investing in the tools for success.* They have no more meaning than sparrows chirping in the sun.

It's another sign, he thinks, and feels a wave of nausea rip through his insides. Since that night, after the bear, after the cops brought his little brother home all snotty and crying because the Handy-Mart didn't have cherry cough candies and so he'd wandered all the way to the Co-op down Inkster and then panicked, Campbell keeps thinking of his cousin George, who would babysit him and his brothers sometimes when his parents went partying.

George is the one who taught Campbell how to tell where he was by looking up and finding the North Star, and how to catch a gopher by laying a small noose over its hole. Now he's in the city, too, and stands in front of the Handy's and plays with himself. Campbell's older brothers beat him up sometimes, in the parking lot or in a back lane, but mostly they try to ignore him. This doesn't always work, and George comes up and shakes Campbell's hand like some businessman on television, and then barks at him like a dog. Just thinking about George has always given him a terrible feeling in his stomach that only really goes away when he's had a few and everybody is relaxed and fooling around. "Crazy George, all right," he says. "The only one of us who doesn't like to take his drugs." And then everybody raises their bottles and says "to Cousin George."

Lately, Campbell hasn't felt like drinking, and the sick feeling is always there. When his older brothers want to party, he knows they know something is wrong because they don't call him little faggot. "What's up, Campy man," they say, "what's with you," but he only shrugs and goes to sit on the front porch, where the breeze feels good against his face. And when his mom looks at him, she doesn't say: "Please, please, please, I don't have time for this shit." She just chews on her lip and then goes away.

"Cam," Debbie whispers, and Campbell jumps. She is crouching right beside him in the dark, and when she laughs, her breath is hot against his ear. He looks at her empty seat, and wonders how she could move with so little sound.

"I didn't mean to startle you," she says, and it's as if her breathing is louder than her voice. Even with his eyes closed, Campbell would know her by her strange, perfumy smell. "I forgot to tell you, when you go up, this man talking now will shake your hand before you speak. So just be ready, okay?"

Campbell doesn't nod right away. For two weeks she came to The Freak to help him write the speech, always wearing something different and smelling the same. Over and over, she asked him about himself, about his family and his goals, and he told her things he wasn't sure were true, but could be. She typed right into a laptop computer balanced on her knees and looked at him the way his mom sometimes did, back when he was small, before she would run her fingers through his hair.

"You're going to blow them away," she'd say, or other things he knew were crap but liked anyway. One time, she surprised him and said something really funny. "Don't be nervous," she said, sitting behind The Freak's pool table and looking like one of those ladies that read the news on TV. "You know, you won't even be able to see all those people, because the room will be dark and you'll be on a stage. Like, if you have a booger hanging from your nose, they won't even notice."

Now, feeling her breath quick and soft, part of him wants to wrap his hands tight around her neck and see what she will do. And part of him wants to pretend he doesn't hear, so she will stay crouched beside him in the dark.

He nods, and she squeezes his arm and sneaks away.

Campbell closes his eyes and concentrates on the man's voice at the microphone. But the words still drift over him, and he hears another man in his head.

"Just a little guy," his dad says. "Poor little shit."

Campbell remembers the first bear he ever saw, lying beside a pile of garbage behind their house. Campbell's mom was holding him and he was crying, not because the bear was dead but because the rifle shot had scared him from sleep.

"Just one taste," his mom said, but she was crying too. "That's all it takes, Campy. We can't have them coming around all the time, eh."

The dead bear, he thinks, that was all the way back when she still cried. He remembers it was very early, barely light, and there was the smell of his mom's bedtime hair and aspens in the morning.

Suddenly there is clapping, and Campbell instinctively joins in. He can hardly feel his hands, but then he hears his name. The dark shape across the table that is Debbie is giving him a wave.

As Campbell eases back his chair, a napkin drops from his lap, but he lets it fall without a thought. Cautiously, one foot in front of the other, he moves through the darkness toward the stage. In his mind, he is watching the black bear run from behind the Santa house, across the street, then where? Where does the fucking thing go in a crowded city?

When he finally gets up to the podium, he is alone. The spotlight is unbelievably bright and he must shield his eyes to look around. Whoever's hand he was supposed to shake has disappeared.

He reaches into his pocket and takes out the folded speech, smoothes it flat on the podium, and stares hard at the paper, trying to forget, just this once, for these few minutes, that he is going crazy.

My name is Campbell Sinclair. I am sixteen years old and I am the second youngest of five brothers.

His mouth feels dry. Though Debbie has printed out the speech in giant letters, the words swim in front of him like tadpoles. He hears her voice, *slow down, slow down and look up,* but all he wants now is to be gone. When the words come back into focus, he does not even take a breath. He just reads.

I spent my childhood in a small Northern community, and came to the city when I was ten. My dad, when he started drinking he couldn't stop, and this created problems for my mom and us kids.

He knows he is going too fast, not pausing in the right spots. But it's like someone has pulled a string in his back and he cannot stop.

We had moved to the city to start again, and it was hard for me. I didn't know anyone, and there are many temptations for a young boy in the inner city. I started going to The Freight House to play pool. I got better and better, and one day, the staff asked me, since I was there all the time, if I wanted to work there and hang out with the smaller kids. I thought, why not, and now I've been working there for two years. The hardest thing to learn was remembering not to swear in front of the younger ones.

There is laughter, and Campbell is momentarily thrown off. His lips stick to his teeth, and his tongue feels huge. Then he remembers that these people can't even see if he has a booger hanging off his nose. They couldn't see if he was drooling, or had a giant oozing scab on his forehead. And Debbie has given him these words that are supposed to blow them away.

He licks his lips and starts reading again, but more slowly now.

I think Freight House has made a big difference in my life. It has given me a safe alternative to the streets, and shown me that there are people who really care. I feel like I'm making a difference now in giving other kids something to do and helping them learn new things. In the future, I hope to graduate from high school and go on to college or university. Mostly, I'm interested in being a lawyer, or starting my own business.

He pauses then, because for a moment, right then, he half-believes this to be true.

I would like to thank my mom, who is my role model. She couldn't be here today because she had to work. I'd also like to thank all of you here today for supporting places like Freight House, and the difference it is making in the lives of inner-city kids. Thank you.

First, there's no sound at all. Then there's a thunder of clapping, loud and rhythmic, and the shapes get bigger and they are standing and clapping some more. It's like a vibration deep inside, like Campbell's bones are rattling. Never in his life has he felt like this. All at once, he sees his mom's tired face and wants to scratch her eyes out for not being here, and he feels a sweet, sweet relief that she is not, that no one he knows has heard that speech.

Out of the corner of his eye, he sees Debbie standing with the minister or the mayor.

"Cam," she shouts. She is practically jumping up and down. "Campbell."

Part of him wants to go to her, to feel her tits as she hugs him and tells him that he is amazing and brave. Part of him does not want to face these people just yet.

He turns back to the big, black room. The light is still blinding, but he doesn't care. He stares straight into it.

In his mind, he is small again. Cousin George, who is still normal as normal can be, is chasing him through the tall grass with a little shovel because Campbell keeps eating all the saskatoon berries meant for his mom's wine.

"Go George, get the little bugger," Campbell's dad shouts, but he's laughing like he used to sometimes, bent almost double.

Campbell is fast. Though the grass scrapes his bare legs and the small stones cut his feet, there is the sweet smell of berries and smoke and sweat. In his mind, he is running fast under the blazing August sun, so happy he's afraid he might explode.

Back Lane Lullaby

Four Facts and a Couple of Superstitions

1. Besides Russia and Ukraine itself, Canada has the largest number of people of Ukrainian origin in the world. Most Ukrainian immigrants were landless peasants who came to settle the Canadian prairies between 1890 and 1920.

2. At the beginning of the twentieth century, Ukraine had one of the fastest population growth rates in Europe. Over the next century, however, Ukrainians had fewer children while death rates grew and life expectancy actually decreased. There were 6 million fewer Ukrainians in 2012 than in 1990.

3. Paul Simon's 1986 hit song "You Can Call Me Al," from his Graceland album, was inspired by an incident at a party where French composer Pierre Boulez mistakenly referred to Paul as "Al." Later, Simon was criticized for not adequately recognizing the contribution of the South African musicians and singers who played a predominant role in the recordings.

4. While we know that 47 workers died as a result of the 1986 nuclear explosion in Chernobyl, Ukraine, the exact long-term death toll remains controversial. Experts estimate that anywhere from 4,000 to nearly a million people have died or will die as a result of their exposure to disaster-related radiation poisoning.

Many traditional Ukrainian superstitions are still alive and well today, such as do not start anything new on a Friday or get your hair cut when a family member is sick.

The Friday night he rang the doorbell it was hot out, maybe thirty degrees, even though July was long gone and school would be starting soon. They weren't expecting anybody, and in Trish's experience when you're not expecting someone, nobody comes, except maybe fundraisers going door-to-door. The three of them were at the kitchen table eating barbecued chicken. Her mother was squinting at how much butter her father was putting on his potato, and her father was explaining what life was like before air conditioning. When the doorbell interrupted him mid-sentence, they all looked at each other, as if they'd never heard such a sound in their lives. And then her father sighed and wiped his fingers and his mouth in the slow, careful way he did a lot of things. And as usual, her mother lost patience and began noisily sliding her chair to get the door herself. But it was Trish who, for some reason, actually said, "I got it."

So it was Trish who found Alexi standing on the doorstep in the thick heat of a late Winnipeg summer. Later, this moment would sometimes fly into her head just before sleep and out again just as quickly, as if it was almost too bizarre to think of as a real memory, as real life. There she was, expecting to see a kid selling chocolate-covered almonds or other junk her father would have a good excuse to eat, and instead she found a sweaty young guy with a gold tooth, who held out a ratty old suitcase like he was giving her a present and said: "I believe this is the residence of one Taras Dudek, and if this is the truth, then I believe you are my cousin."

And all Trish could do was stare stupidly. "Dad," she yelled. "I think it's for you."

Looking at it from the outside, of course, it wasn't really *that* bizarre. Her father's name was in fact Taras, a common name for Canadian-Ukrainian boys on account of the great Taras Shevchenko, whose tragic, old poems Trish knew by rote because she spent every Saturday morning of her childhood in a church basement learning what a suffering hero he was. Though Trish's parents were both born in Winnipeg, she knew all about how her Ukrainian ancestors had suffered under the Poles or the Romanians or the Russian communists for centuries on end. And the Dudeks did in fact keep in contact with several distant relatives there, including Trish's grandmother's two half-sisters. Every six months or so, Trish's family would go to Baba Dudek's, and together they'd pack tea and tampons and other boring things, along with some crisp American twenty-dollar bills, into a large box addressed to the capital city of Kiev. The last time they'd done it, her baba had pointed at Trish like a gypsy sending out a warning, and said something like: "You be glad I came here, so you can be a proud Ukrainian. Over there, they still don't have nothing. The communists are gone but now there is nothing but criminals. Honest people have to live eleven people, in-laws and all, in four rooms. What do you think of that, you an only child in that big house? Eh?"

As usual, this left Trish slightly unsettled. When she listened to her baba, part of her always felt like she should try to figure out what her baba was talking about, because somewhere in the complaining and lecturing and gossip, there was something that was somehow important. But the other part of her, the bigger part, felt like the only way she could stand to be with her baba, or even love her, was if she just let it all go in one ear and out the other.

There was no ignoring, however, the strange, sweaty guy at the door. There he was, one of her baba's half-sisters' granddaughter's cousins, stopping in for a visit on his way to see a business associate in Chicago.

"I, Alexi, am also a businessman," he said, now standing and sweating in the Dudeks' front hall. By this time, Trish was holding his suitcase by a handle that was barely attached. She couldn't stop staring like an idiot, and her father wasn't much better, just rocking back and forth on his heels, as he always did when he was trying to make small talk at weddings or funerals.

Trish decided that Alexi didn't look any older than her real cousin, Darryl, who was twenty-two. His clothes were brand new—bright, white cross-trainers, dark blue jeans, and a Calvin Klein T-shirt you could tell had never been washed because the sleeves still showed sharp creases in the cotton.

"So sorry, Alexi," her mother said, reappearing from the kitchen with a tea towel. "Chicken can be so messy." She spoke in Ukrainian with her ultra-friendly and polite voice. "So tell us, Alexi, what business are you in?"

Alexi flashed his gold tooth. "I am a businessman, who is a family man as well," he replied in English. Everything about his face was round and soft, except for the sharp, almost eerie blue eyes that seemed to be soaking up not just the front hallway, but the whole living room and family room and kitchen. When he spoke, Trish could not help noticing that his breath smelled bad.

"This is why I thought why not come and take time to see the family in the Winnipeg."

This finally seemed to jolt her father into action. "Well, come in, come in," he said.

"If we'd known you were coming," her mother added, "we'd have picked you up at the airport." Then she grabbed the suitcase from Trish and the handle ripped right off. The case went *thump* at their feet, and her mother stared at it as if she had no idea how they were ever going to get the thing into the house now. Trish knew she was probably distracted, trying to remember when the sheets on the spare bed were changed last, even though Alexi didn't look like the type to care.

"That is broken," he said, sitting in her father's recliner and grinning. "No worries. And please, I prefer English, not Ukrainian, so English please. My friends, they call me Al. Like Paul Simon. You can call me Al. You know?"

Trish watched for her parents' reaction. Nothing in her experience had prepared her for someone from Ukraine who listened to her parents' eighties music and didn't want to speak his own language. Her father gave Alexi what she had come to recognize as his vice-principal-face. Since she'd been about twelve, she'd noticed his mouth would take on a special shape before he talked seriously with one of his students. "I am your friend," it said, "and I am your superior."

Her mother was already heading back to the kitchen.

"Paul Simon. Yes, of course," she said over her shoulder, still in Ukrainian. "But let me get you something, Alexi. When was the last time you ate?"

He shrugged, and shouted in English, "Please, no trouble."

Trish's father sank down into the couch. "Ukrainian is fine, you know. We're all comfortable with it." His mouth eased into his proud-papa grin. "It's Patricia's second language but her grammar is better than my mother's."

Alexi spun around to Trish and waved her in, as if it was his house instead of hers. "Patrooosia, eh?" he said, pronouncing her name in Ukrainian. He stretched the middle syllable like an owl hooting in the night. "So my little cousin is Patrooosia, the most beautiful Ukrainian name. But it's Russian or English for me."

That's when he pulled out a package of cigarettes and waved it at her father. "When I was a little one, it was Russian in school, and now English is the words of business." He shrugged and put a cigarette to his lips. "Nothing but English."

Trish's father tried not to show his displeasure at the mention of Putin's Russia, but his grin grew smaller and more determined. Her mother came in carrying iced tea and cookies and she stared at the unlit cigarette like Alexi had just grown a second nose. Still, her voice was all politeness.

In Ukrainian, she said: "How long are you planning to be in Winnipeg?"

"Uh, few months," Alexi answered in English, then laughed until the cigarette fell from his lips. "No, no, I mean, few weeks, maybe." Holding up his hands at the tray, he spluttered. "Please, I please you, none for me. If I speak truthfully, I would like right now more than anything to have this smoke and then bed. My time, it is all off, and I feel so sleepy my English is not so good."

So the evening ended with Alexi smoking in their backyard while Trish's mother changed the spare bed sheets.

In her own bed that night, Trish couldn't stop thinking about things, like how someone who looked so hot could turn down iced tea. Or what Alexi must have thought when he stood smoking by their pool and the rock garden and the cedar gazebo that Baba Dudek called "that fancy, screened shack." Or why, when her parents whispered about how wonderful it was that Alexi had miraculously raised enough money to escape the corruption and political chaos of Ukraine, and that he seemed like a nice boy with ambition, it felt as if they were trying to convince themselves that this was true.

Gradually, though, these thoughts became merely words running through her head, like *bad, bad breath*, and *blue, blue eyes*, and the next thing she knew, it was Saturday morning and she was gasping for air.

Trish was not used to waking up in a state of panic because

her dreams were almost always boring or stupid. When she tried to remember them, they were usually something like her science teacher standing by their pool, telling her she'd missed a midterm, and then blowing his nose exactly like her Aunt Syl. This time, though, she could not catch her breath, so she lay back on her damp pillow and tried hard to bring the dream back.

She'd been sitting by the pool with her friend Tonya, whose father was their Orthodox priest, and who competed with Trish for who could get the best marks, or pour the most tea at the reliably lame Easter luncheon. In the dream, she was mad at Trish for some reason and said in Ukrainian, "No wonder they always called you Sucky Trishy," which was what Dale Golding called her in grade two just to be a little jerk. Then Alexi walked up and offered Trish a cigarette. Tonya said, "Your parents are going to like kill you," and disappeared, and then Trish and Alexi were dangling their feet in the water and she was smoking like she'd been doing it her whole life. "This is really bad for you," she said. Alexi laughed and said, "Many, many things are bad for you, Patrooosia." Then she started coughing and spluttering and that was it.

Fully awake now, Trish realized she'd been hearing the shower running for a long time.

There was a knock on her door. "Ten-thirty, up and at 'em," her dad said. "If Alexi ever gets out of the shower, he wants to see Wal-Mart and then we're having lunch at Baba's."

All Trish wanted was to roll over and sleep some more. But she knew her mom wouldn't even knock. No matter how many times Trish asked her not to, her mom would come right into her room and open the blinds. So Trish rolled out and got dressed.

They were all ready and waiting in the van when Alexi came through the back gate, not quite finished his cigarette. His hair was still wet and slicked back like a TV gangster's. Trish didn't think it suited his round face. He was wearing the same clothes as yesterday, and already sweating a little.

"Good morning to you," he said, climbing in beside her. "In Ukraine, you know, Patrooosia, where I come from, they would make cars like out of tin, so when you are hit, squash, you're dead." He flashed his gold tooth like he thought this was funny. "In Chicago, I will buy a Lexus with a roof that opens."

In the rear-view mirror, Trish could see her father's vice-principal-face. "A Lex, eh? I hope your friend in Chicago is doing really well."

Alexi shrugged and smiled at Trish as if they were sharing a joke.

At Wal-Mart, though, there was no smiling. It was like none of them even existed. Alexi just kept picking up stuff and putting it down with a very serious look. In the end, all he bought was some caramel corn in a giant tin with racehorses on it, and a large bag of white sweat socks. When her dad tried to pay, as a "welcome to Canada" gift, Alexi waved him away. "I got it covered," he kept saying. "I got it covered."

For most of the way to Baba Dudek's, Alexi and her father babbled on about different kinds of cars. But the closer they got to her baba's, where the houses were old or abandoned or even boarded up, the quieter Alexi got. Trish could feel his blue eyes soaking things up. At the corner of her baba's street, she noticed something was different.

"The dry cleaning place burnt," she said.

Her father nodded and stared straight ahead. "They should clean that up. It's been more than a month."

At the corner, a big black dog with no collar veered off the boulevard and into traffic, as if on a suicide mission. Trish's father swerved, nearly broadsiding a filthy white van in the next lane.

"It's a goddam zoo," he murmured. Trish's mother put her hand on his thigh and squeezed.

Alexi shook his head solemnly. "We are like the dogs," he said. "We want the freedom, but we need the collar to save us from our own selves."

As they pulled up to the house, Alexi leaned forward. He was close enough to whisper in her father's ear. "Here, where your mother lives," he said, "it is poor conditions."

No one said a word as they unbuckled themselves and got out of the van. Her father slammed the door and looked at Alexi with a face that Trish didn't recognize. His cheeks were red and stretched. "It's been going downhill for fifty years, but she won't move."

Alexi crinkled his nose, as if he didn't quite understand, or smelled something bad.

"She can be a stubborn woman," her mother added.

Suddenly everybody seemed to be in a bad mood, except for Baba Dudek, who was coming down the front walk, shuffling pretty fast for an old lady who weighed over two hundred pounds.

"Come in, come in," she said in Ukrainian, grabbing Alexi's arm as if she was afraid he'd run away. When he handed her the giant tin of caramel corn, she acted like it was the best present she'd ever had, better than the TV or microwave or other big things Trish's family would usually get her for Christmas.

She led them to her tiny back yard and practically pushed Alexi into an old lawn chair. "Sit, sit," she said. Most of Baba's yard was a vegetable garden, scattered with plastic pails. Trish and her parents sat on the rotting wooden storage bench that Trish's mother called "that old coffin of hers."

Baba Dudek stood right over poor Alexi, breathing hard from the excitement. "I was the oldest sister," she said. "And you are the first one to come see me. At least that has changed." Her fat body shaded Alexi's face. "Is it as bad there as they say? When I left, many, many years ago, people were poor, but honest. The fields were more beautiful than anything in the world. Now they say everything is ruined."

Alexi shrugged. "Your relatives are well," he said in Ukrainian, "and they send you good wishes."

Baba Dudek nodded and licked her lips. Her eyes were watery and blank. When she turned to Trish and her parents, it was as if she didn't even see them. "And you've already met my son and his family," she said, still staring into space. "Taras is a vice-principal at the university and Evelyn a teacher. Of course, you have already seen their house."

Alexi put a cigarette in his mouth and said, "It's a nice house."

"It's a high school at the university," Trish's father said. "The Collegiate."

Baba Dudek glared at him. "That's what I said."

Then she licked her lips again and ran her hand over Alexi's head. "But let me look at you. You're a nice-looking boy. Still have your hair. But you wouldn't have been born when the radiation exploded all over, eh."

It took Trish a moment to remember what her baba was talking about—the nuclear accident at Chernobyl back in the 1980s.

Alexi lit his cigarette and grinned for the first time since getting in the van. "We kids, we had a game," he said, still in Ukrainian. "We would play radiation monster. You know, years after Chernobyl we had Geiger counters to test for radiation levels, so those were our magic swords…" He trailed off then, his blue eyes focused somewhere next door. "Real Indians!" he yelled in English.

Everyone turned to see Baba Dudek's neighbour, Irene, and her family, piling into their van. All the Traverses, young and old, were dressed in traditional Aboriginal regalia, the boys complete with headdresses.

Trish lifted her arm to wave, but immediately felt stupid because she barely recognized any of them now. When she was small, she had sometimes played with the Traverse kids who were around her age—usually tag, or statues, or just goofing around—while her mother peered from behind the curtains in the front window. They were always there when they drove up to Baba Dudek's and there when they left, as if they played outside forever and never even went in to drink or sleep. Their clothes usually smelled sweet, like grass and sweat and fabric softener rolled into one, and sometimes they did crazy things, like eat a bug just to see what it tasted like. Elmer, the oldest, had jumped off the roof for fun.

Baba Dudek nodded knowingly. "They're going to a pow-wow." Then she turned to Alexi. "The Indians, they like to dance but not to work hard."

Trish tried to ignore her comment, hoping Alexi wouldn't understand. But her mother threw her head back. "Mama Dudek, you know that's not true."

Baba Dudek became the crazy gypsy again, wagging her crooked finger at Trish's mother. "Irene is my friend. I can say what I want."

Alexi didn't seem to hear any of it. He was completely cheered up now, jumping up and down to get a better look. "Like the movies. This is why you come to Canada, no? To see the real Indians! Do you see the feathers? Real feathers!"

And no matter how hard Trish tried over lunch, and all the way home, to convince Alexi that the Traverses did not normally dress like that, that a powwow was a special occasion, that they were just normal people, he would only smile and shake his head. "Okay, okay," he finally said, flashing his gold tooth and winking as if to humour her. "Maybe this is so. But, Patrooosia, I saw them for myself. They were the real Indians. They look like in the movies. For real."

When they got home, Trish felt so tired all she wanted was to go to her room, maybe text her friend Tonya. But Alexi was like a wind-up toy, pacing up and down the hall, sticking his head in her doorway and smiling wordlessly before he was off again. Finally he paused long enough to ask if there were "clubs, for the dancing, you know?" Something in the way he swivelled his hips made her embarrassed that she had no real idea what was available.

"Aah, sweet little Patrooosia," he whispered, as if they were in on this together. "You are so fine I forget you are still just a girl. I go ask your daddy. He looks like a man who can shake it, eh."

Much to her surprise, Trish's father agreed to drop Alexi off downtown, with instructions to call when he was ready to come home.

And when she finally texted Tonya, she didn't mention Alexi at all. Instead they talked about everyday things that had nothing to do with Indians or Ukrainians.

When Trish came down to breakfast the next morning, her parents were in a state because Alexi hadn't called. They asked if he'd mentioned any other plans to her, and when she said no, they looked at each other, then back at her, purposefully, as if she might be lying.

"Why would he tell *me* anything?" she asked.

They didn't hear from him until the police brought him home in the middle of the afternoon. He'd tried to shoplift a game console from the Wal-Mart. Trish's father talked quietly with the young female police officer in the kitchen while Alexi stood in the front hall. His white Calvin Klein T-shirt was dirty now with what looked like mustard, and his blue eyes seemed completely absorbed by his shoes. After fifteen minutes, the police officer left. She brushed passed Alexi and held up a finger. "You get one break here. So stay out of trouble."

Then her father looked at him with the same strange face he'd had when they pulled up to Baba Dudek's, his cheeks red and strained. "I'm sorry, Alexi. Trish is fifteen. We can't have the police here. You'll have to leave."

Alexi didn't say anything, just went straight to the spare bedroom to get his broken suitcase.

Before he left, he stopped in Trish's room to say goodbye. "I'm off to Chicago to see my businessman."

Trish looked up from her magazine. Just like the time she'd first seen him, all she could do was nod like an idiot.

Alexi stood in the doorway silently, his suitcase at his feet, like he was hoping she'd start talking and he wouldn't have to leave. Then he reached for the iPad on her desk. He turned it over as if he was inspecting it for defects. "This is yours, yes?"

She nodded some more.

He fixed his sharp blue eyes on her as if he was going to share some profound secret. "You know, when I was small boy, nobody in my country could even play the CDs. The stores, they were empty. Now, the shelves are full, but you must be a thief to buy. There is no money. You see?"

Trish didn't know what was the matter with her, but all she could do was nod.

Part of her couldn't help thinking Alexi wanted her to give him the iPad, as a *farewell from Canada* present or something. And she felt as if he was trying to make her feel sorry for him, to manipulate her. Because maybe he was a liar, maybe there was no businessman from Chicago at all.

And another part of her suddenly hated her parents, madly and passionately, more than she'd ever hated the stupid things Baba Dudek said. There they were, the big, proud Ukrainian-Canadians, actually kind of relieved that he was leaving their nice, clean spare room. They were hypocrites, complaining about the "challenge" of Asian students taking over the Collegiate even though foreign tuitions paid for their cushy pensions.

They took things for granted. They took her for granted. Like how could her mom barge into her room in the morning like she was five? And why did they always assume she would just come along with them? What if she'd had plans yesterday? She hadn't really, but what if she had?

Trish kept nodding. Alexi carefully placed the iPad back on the desk.

"It was pleasure to meet you, Patrooosia."

It took every ounce of energy for Trish to find her voice. For some reason she could not name, she felt ashamed.

"You too, Al," she said.

And then he flashed his gold tooth and was gone.

The next morning, she woke up before her alarm. She was crying a little, but felt very calm, her breathing slow and even. There, in the soft light of seven o'clock, it was as if there was something only her sleepy brain could see, could somehow understand, but it was too late, because Alexi was never coming back.

In the dream, it had been raining earbuds, and she and Alexi were running to escape them. The next thing she knew, they were sitting on her baba's rotting old coffin. They were both soaking wet and then his head was in Trish's lap and she was stroking his slicked-back hair. Very quietly, she whispered a song that she did not recognize, as if she was a mother humming a lullaby even though she was fifteen-and-a-half and he was maybe twenty-two. Somewhere in the background, Baba Dudek was watching them and crying softly. Never in her life had Trish seen her baba cry. It made her look so old, but like a little girl, too. On and on Trish whispered, until Alexi closed his eyes and smiled the way he had when he saw his real Indians.

Her iPad alarm went off, blasting the familiar chorus of the latest number one. She was already a little sick of it. Tonya's voice rang in her ears: "Track starts tomorrow, bright and early. Watch your back this year. I've been cross-training."

Trish didn't just hit snooze; she switched things to *off*. She played the dream over and over in her mind, whispering the lullaby, comforting Alexi and her baba until she fell back to sleep.

Life on Ice

Five Facts

1. Icelanders were the first European visitors to what is now Canada. The first European born in Canada was probably an Icelander, too.
2. Due to their unique colour and expressive faces, belugas are one of the most common whales to be held captive in aquariums around the world.
3. In Reykjavik, Iceland, there is an Elf School which boasts a full curriculum devoted to the study of elves and "hidden people."
4. Icelanders are known for going to the movies more often than any other nation.
5. Churchill is a coastal town that does not benefit from a maritime moderation of winter temperature. The shallow Hudson Bay freezes in fall and prevailing winds from the North Pole jet across the ice and chill it to a -27C average.

No one tells me beforehand about Gordon's Chinese exchange students. My mother just sends me a plane ticket, says I can stay at his place in Winnipeg for the school year.

"Churchill is no place for a young woman. You need a change of scenery," says the Queen of Cliché. "A change is as good as a rest."

Neither of us mentions that I could stay with her if she didn't live in a one-bedroom loft with nice views of the river.

"I'm well rested," I say.

"You know what I mean. You'll meet new people, take different courses—photography, psychology, American poetry..." She trails off, probably already bored with the conversation.

My godfather Gordon has known me my whole life and laughs at his own jokes, like when he introduces himself as my god-fairy. He says humour puts people at ease about the whole homo thing, and he may be right, but he thinks he's funnier than he is. He has a big old house that some famous artist grew up in and spends "the bloody winter" in Arizona, so I guess it should be no great surprise he decided to take in boarders.

"This is *Hi Ho, Hee Haw*, and *Kaploo-ee*," he says when I arrive. Not really, but that's what I hear because I'm surprised and I'm still getting used to the claustrophobic trees.

Gordon's neighbourhood is nothing but three-storey houses built for more kids than people have these days and massive elms that roof in the streets. Where I come from, trees grow stunted, like they started smoking too young, and pre-fab buildings squat naked and exposed, next to nothing but ancient rock and Arctic shoreline. One time, an American tourist got off the train, squinted into the useless sun and exclaimed, "Oh my! It's a trailer park amongst the bears!"

Of course, I wasn't actually there, never heard her myself, so who knows.

"They're just a bit older than you," Gordon says, gesturing grandly towards the boarders like a game-show hostess. "You'll be at the Collegiate in a few weeks and they'll be a stone's throw away at the university."

I haven't actually stayed at Gordon's since I was a kid and recovering from a case of strep gone wrong. It's like he still thinks I'm six. *You kids are almost the same age and you both like ice cream. Isn't that fun?*

I wonder how much anyone has told him. If he's talked to my father, he's probably heard I'm going through some "adolescent thing." My mother would've told him she's worried about my mental health. Either way, he must be aware of my recent "truancy," as the school called it. Truant doesn't sound like the right word for skipping the last two months of school. It sounds too positive, as if it should describe someone antsy for the truth.

Mr. Smythe, my science teacher/guidance counsellor, would've told him that the good-cop approach generally works best in these kinds of situations. "We're not actually angry with you," he'd assured me a few weeks ago. "We're more concerned than anything else. You're on track for university, Jazz. Don't you want to graduate with your friends next year?"

He'd sighed, like I was making a difficult job more difficult. "We need you to talk to us."

There were teensy black dots on his front teeth, up near the gums. He'd probably eaten lunch at Gypsy's, had the honey-and-poppyseed slice. "Has something happened, Jazz?"

Quit saying my name like that, I wanted to say. *Go brush your teeth. I'm just a graduation statistic to you.*

No. Yes. I don't know.

My mother is probably feeling secretly vindicated, had always half-suspected it was only a matter of time before I cracked. They used to say the Inuit managed scarce food supplies by abandoning their old and infirm on ice floes, leaving them to fend for themselves until the inevitable occurred. Maybe that's what my mother had in mind all those years ago, leaving anxious Jasmine with her lazy father and moving on to hardier members of the tribe.

After about a week, I start calling them Ping, Ling, and Sing in my head. Real names are hardly necessary since most of our interactions involve them smiling politely and saying "e-soos me."

Waiting for the bathroom in the morning, Ping finally emerges: "e-soos me." Ling comes to unload the dishwasher while I'm looking in the fridge: "e-soos me." Sing shuts his laptop as I enter the den: "e-soos me." The house is in flames and we're tripping over each other to get the hell out: "e-soos me!" they all shout.

Okay, that last one didn't happen, but that's probably what they'd say. Ping weighs maybe ninety pounds, a good ten of that her impossibly thick, long, glossy hair. She has thin lips and small, slightly crooked teeth but it kind of works. Ling is by no means curvy and I could probably crush her between my thighs if I had to, but she's got a little more meat. Her hair is cut spiky and she wears baby-doll dresses with black high-tops. Sing is basically the male version of the girls: small, attractive, dressed kind of like a cartoon character. They've apparently come here to learn English at the university, but as far as I can tell, they spend all their time talking to each other in Chinese with the odd English brand name thrown in.

When I have nothing to do, which is pretty much always, I imagine taking them back home for a few days. They are so compact, so conscious of space—what do the Asian multitudes make of the tundra's awful emptiness? At one of the souvenir shacks back home they have a TV amongst the shelves of mass-produced mukluks and plastic inukshuks where they show a video of us kids going out for Halloween. It went viral for a while: there we are, barely breathing in our princess dresses or superhero tights yanked over snowsuits, our tiaras and wigs hugging woollen toques, running door-to-door in the height of bear season. The Japanese tourists always stood at the TV and giggled at the craziness of our parents circling in their ATVs, rifles at the ready in case a migrating bear on its way to the coastal ice decided to carry off a sugar-sticky little human. It really is crazy, if you think about it. Like what must the Chinese workers in all those gigantic factories think of the weird shit they have to make for us? Somebody who has no idea about Halloween actually paints those plastic skulls on stakes and funny tombstones we stick in our lawns. Some Buddhist actually sews those Christmas stockings decorated with X-rated elves. What must they think of us? I want to ask the cartoon exchange students but I'm afraid they'll just grin politely, say *e-soos-me, but my English still not much good.*

Ari told me about those X-rated stockings when Frida was away. They're part of his collection of *kitsch*, a word he likes a lot. According to him, the factory-made stuff sold in Churchill was *kitsch*. The vampire books I read were *kitsch*. The Winnie-the-Pooh nightlight I gave to baby Elizabet was the sweetest thing because it used to be mine, but it was still *kitsch*.

I try to get their voices out of my head, have tried for weeks, for months, since Ari and Frida and their little Elizabet left for good in May, but I'm a complete and utter failure.

Frida is half in love with you, Ari says. *You remind her of herself when you were her age, and no one loves Frida like Frida.*

Wear your hair down, Frida says, *don't straighten it. Leave your hair to its own devices and you're a panther girl.*

Even fat-faced Elizabet still babbles at me. *Ja, Ja, Ja. Come Ja. Come.*

I start following the comings and goings of the Chinese students probably more than is healthy. It turns out there is no *exchange* going on. No Winnipeg contingent will be travelling to China to learn calligraphy and Confucius.

"Their parents are businesspeople," Gordon says matter-of-factly, "usually with good Party connections, which is why they're here and can pay."

I eat my raisin toast very, very, very slowly as they heat up their strange, fishy-smelling breakfasts. Every few days, Gordon drives them to a take-out Asian market in the West End to stock up because he's a keener that way, always wanting to show how worldly he is, and because none of them really seems to know how to cook. Ping is obviously the only one with a clue and is in charge of boiling the sticky rice they eat with pretty much everything. Except supper, when Gordon prepares quesadillas or farmer sausage and mashed potatoes or bacon and mushroom omelets to let them experience Western cuisine. Sing speaks the best English and manages to tell us that Ling refuses to eat anything with cheese because it smells like "foot."

With a little spying, I learn Ping has begun wasting a lot of time playing computer solitaire. I learn that when Ling thinks she's alone, she does the same funky dance as soon as her earbuds are in. I learn that Sing goes through expensive hair gel as fast as his vitamin water and seems totally oblivious to Gordon smiling at him from across the room.

Sometimes I even write these things down in a spiral-bound notebook because when I was a kid, they called me sensitive but as I got older, they started throwing around "obsessive-compulsive."

Dear Frida: Gordon says "The West End" like he lives in London instead of a two-bit prairie 'burb. Ping is left-handed and almost certainly the one who snores. Ling doesn't make her bed but spends approximately twenty minutes making her hair look like she just woke up. Sing knows more English than he lets on. Shyness? Lechery?

My dad never mentioned the big O-C, just said I took things too hard. Like the time our town lost Lonnie Harper to high tide and I refused to go anywhere near the water for over a year. I kept thinking of his squinchy little Harper face, his big Harper ears, his dumb ol' Harper bravado daring to brave the waves until *swoosh*, he was gone, swallowed up by the icy water as if he'd never existed, like the Harper clan had never had a little boy about my age, with a quarter-sized birthmark, red as raw meat, on his right cheek.

"You gotta come back on the boat with me sometime," my dad said. "Getting a babysitter is getting expensive." But I was a kid and didn't give two shits about his business. Let someone else take the tourists out into the Bay so they could squeal at the beluga whale families who swam by in a flash of white streaks, beautiful and fleeting enough to taunt us. I wasn't going anywhere. I wouldn't let him fill the bathtub past three inches.

Maybe that's why when I stopped going to school, my dad could barely bring himself to care. When my best friend William moved south in grade five, I cried every morning for months, refused to eat any of his favourite foods, saved up my allowance for a flight to Winnipeg for so long that dear William pretty much forgot who I was. When my friend Amber's dad got transferred to Nunavut, I played Sim City every night, from seven until ten-thirty, for approximately a year.

After a while, my dad must've grown complacent with my extremes, couldn't be bothered to get his panties all in a knot over the inevitable.

"Jesus, Ken," my mother once said. "Sometimes it's like I have to poke you with a stick to see if you're alive."

Dear Frida: Ping chews her nails and spits them wherever. Ling burps little dainty burps after she eats and no one seems to notice but me. Maybe Sing does notice Gordon's puppy-dog smiles. Maybe Dad is more extreme than he thinks: who else is so stubbornly, relentlessly, obsessively contented?

After two weeks in Little China, my mother comes by to take me out to lunch, her pick, of course. Gordon must've told her I wasn't leaving the house.

"So, hon, you ready for next week? We should go shopping, get you some new jeans."

The sushi place is way across the tracks in the North End of town, which I'm sure my mother believes makes the food extra authentic. It's decorated in Japanese kitsch, and some kind of dreary lute music is wafting in through hidden speakers. I can't be bothered to feign enthusiasm. "That would be nice."

"Come on, Jasmine," my mother says. "Don't be like that. You're here, let's have some fun."

"What?" I ask. "I said it would be nice."

She holds up her hands as if surrendering, waves them around. She is thin, looks good for her age, but the skin beneath her biceps has gone slack and flabby. "Okay, okay. Let's have a nice lunch."

"Dad's coming down tomorrow," I say.

The theatrics are over. Her thin lips tighten into a smile and I recognize the lipstick—she'd sent me Positively Plum with a brief note: *Thought you might like to try this—it suits our colouring.* She laughs, but her eyes don't even crinkle at the corners. "What did you do to drag him down here?"

My dad has never liked to fly, says it feels unnatural to him, so he'll take the all-day train to Thompson, then rent a car and drive all night to Winnipeg. I shrug, like a cheeky teenager on TV who's denying all responsibility. "He's just coming."

"I worry, you know," she says. "I worry he's made you into too much of a homebody. I have no regrets except that."

She sees no contradiction in critiquing Dad's parenting, even though she gave up custody ages ago. A *small town is a good place to grow up, she likes to say. Just ask me, or Gordon, or your dad.* The three of us had a childhood you only read about in storybooks these days. She can talk herself into just about anything, beelining out of the North pretty much right after Gordon, leaving Dad and the "village" to raise me, conveniently settling into a one-bedroom place, then thinking she did me some kind of favour by leaving me up in Churchill. That she still has some kind of say.

What makes it worse, or maybe better, I don't know, is that I'm convinced she loves me. And no matter what I do, she will still love me, would come to the courtroom after I'd murdered somebody, hold up a sign that said MY BABY IS INNOCENT! It's just the day-to-day she can't handle, the hands-on nuts and bolts of being there for someone.

When the waitress comes, my mother asks me what kind of bubble tea I want. She squeezes my hand across the table, like she knows she's crossed some kind of line. "Tell me about the babysitting you were doing. Gordon tells me they were from Greenland or something."

I have no memory of telling Gordon about Ari and Frida, but who knows. I may have mentioned something because he has a way of wheedling things out of you. He's such a people-person, so friendly, so interested, and so dangerous, because you never know what he'll share or with whom.

"Iceland," I say.

My mother does not release my hand. "That's right. Iceland. Tell me about them."

Frida wears the kind of sheer bras that let your nipples peak through.

Ari smells like firewood and electrical tape.

I take a long, leisurely sip of mango tea and give her the facts, the straight facts, so help me god.

I tell her a documentary crew came in April, almost too late in the season to get any decent footage of the aurora borealis. Ari was the sound technician, Frida was his wife, a textile artist, and Elizabet was their adorable fat baby, eighteen months old, just starting to walk because of her heft. They rented the place across the street for a couple of months. I helped them out.

Feel this wool, Frida says, *dig your fingers right in, Jasmine. I lugged it here because I can't live without it. Everything I make must have this, this odd mixture of rough softness. This wool, so sweet-smelling when it's dry, turns quite vile when it's wet. I love it and I hate it, and that's why I love it.*

"So you earned yourself some money," my mother says. "That must've felt good."

I know she's striving not to bring up my truancy, trying to make this a nice lunch. I don't tell her that Ari and Frida could barely feed themselves and Elizabet, never mind hire a nanny. I don't tell her that Frida means fair and beautiful and that Ari means eagle.

Look at her eat, Jasmine, Ari says. *Look at my rosy girl eat with such joy. We should all feel such joy, huh? Watch her, and don't forget such joy.*

I nod at my mother, pretend I'm too busy sucking the dregs of the bubble tea.

"Is your dad coming to see you at Gordon's?" she asks.

She likes to insinuate that my dad is a racist homophobe. All I know is that my dad never mentions anyone's sexuality—hetero, homo, bi, two-spirited, or trans—and hasn't spoken to Gordon in years. All I know is that even if my dad tells the odd racist joke, he has two friends in town and one of them is Dene. It's like opposites attracted with my parents, and it was great, until it wasn't. For years, in Swan River, better known as The-Middle-of-Nowhere, Manitoba, Gordon, Ken, and Sandra were the Fab Three, always together. Until Gordon decided he needed to be somewhere he could let his fag flag fly. Until my dad decided his temperament was better suited to the Polar Bear Capital of the World. Until my mother decided she needed to follow her dream and become the executive assistant to a mid-size university's dean of arts.

I remove my sweaty hand from beneath hers. "I guess so."

I made fresh buns, Frida says. *Come over and eat some. Ari is always happier with young people. He likes to play the sage.*

You like my beard? Ari asks. I see you looking. You want to touch it? Elizabet yanks away, don't worry. It took two years to be like this, a golden grizzly man. It's so fine I worry that one night Frida will shave me in my sleep and steal it for her art.

A group of all-ages Japanese, probably an extended family, file into the restaurant and a big black dog nearly follows them. The grandma closes the door in his furry face and the kids giggle to each other. My mother refreshes her Positively Plum and looks around for our waitress. "Oh, did I tell you about the young man who spoke at our AGM?"

I must have a stupid look on my face, because she explains. "Our annual general meeting. It's a lunch at the convention centre."

I remember now. She's gotten all charitable, but not doling out soup and coffee at a church kitchen or anything. She's representing the university on some big charity's board of directors.

"Anyway, you should've seen this inner-city kid who goes to a youth drop-in centre get up in front of a thousand people, every

who's who in the city. Life handed him nothing and there he was, bringing the mayor to his feet."
"Sounds great," I say.
"Be nice," she says. "This has been nice, no? A nice lunch?"
"I said it was great," I say.

Dear Frida: My mother believes I'm going to emerge from all this like some kind of conquering heroine—better, stronger, with many important lessons learned. But I bet you any money she'd lock her car doors if she saw that triumphant young man on the street.

I wake up to Gordon lecturing the three —Ings. Last night, he apparently saw them crossing the street against the light, right into traffic.
"I know back home you must do that, but drivers expect it, because there's no other way. But here, we have crosswalks, we have lights to guide who goes when. Drivers don't expect you to risk your life just to get to the other side." He sounds shaken up. For the first time, I wonder if Gordon ever feels bad that he didn't have kids. He lived with this guy Samuel for a few years, until Samuel left to do his doctoral thesis in Montreal and didn't invite Gordon along.

Dear Frida: Every morning, the —Ings watch Gordon doing tai chi in the yard. They all laugh their little "e-soos me" laughs but only Ping cups her hand over her mouth, as usual.

I go get some juice from the fridge, still in my ratty sleep T-shirt that says I Hate Mondays.
"Look who decided to join the land of the living," Gordon says.
The —Ings e-soos themselves, chastised and repentant, beg

off to do whatever dutiful Asian hipsters do when they leave the house and head into traffic.

Gordon drapes his arm around me, kisses the top of my head. "You okay, kid? You ready to head back to school? Tell your godfairy what's on your mind."

Did you know, Jasmine, Frida says, *we Icelanders, we have the purest genetic makeup of any nation on earth. We're all interbred. Ari and I, we're probably cousins back somewhere not too far.*

Jasmine. I love this name on you, Ari says. *Your parents, so young, not ready to settle for Canadian names. They must have thought it sounded like the East, so different, so romantic. It's kitsch, you know, but I love it.*

I spin from beneath Gordon's arm, pretend I hate him treating me like a baby. "Just enjoying your hospitality," I say. "You could've been a chef in another life."

"Your dad almost went to cooking school, you know," Gordon says. "He worked short order while we were in school. But then he moved to the tundra, where humans are not meant to live because food does not grow there."

"What about the Inuit?" I ask.

He puts his hands on his hips, Queen of the queens. "You want to eat blubber? And don't change the subject. We're talking about you."

He tells me that he understands, he really does, I'm having a tough time, it's a tough age, but I'll see, I'm no longer stuck in the big chill, the world will open before me in a few weeks. There'll be new sights, new people, new interests. A new start.

I know he's right, that it's a crying shame Gordon will never have kids of his own. I know my dad will re-enter civilization, will wander around the campus with me, will want to show me how much he cares. I know my mother will take me shopping, whip out her gold credit card, ask me if I'm having a good time.

But after Gordon leaves for yoga, I lie around the empty house beneath the towering trees, hating every member of the Fab Three, waiting for the —Ings to return, waiting for something to distract me from my dread.

The pot is empty, the film is quit, Ari says. *What do the dancing lights care about our lack of money? What do the stars care about our little problems? We'll go back to our bankrupt country and nurse our wounds with bread and homemade whiskey.*

When I think of this place, Jasmine, I will always think of you, and the smiling whales, Frida says. *Those whales, they look so white, so stupidly innocent, but really, they are smart. Whales are smart. You, Jasmine, you are young, you've seen so little, but you are smart. You and the whales, Jasmine.*

Ja, Ja, Elizabet says. *Ja, come.*

Dear Frida: Do you hate me?

I go over the facts, just the facts, so help me god.

Frida left first, flew down to the artists' festival on the rocky shores of Lake Winnipeg that remind Icelanders of home. She took Elizabet because people are more likely to buy art when they see a chubby mouth to feed. She kissed me goodbye on both cheeks, made me promise that we would *stay in each other's orbits*. Elizabet played shy, like she knew I would be a stranger soon enough. Ari stayed to finish up, to vacuum-pack giant bags of Frida's fabric for transport.

The next day, or the next, I don't know, Ari called me over just before bed, said he'd made vinarterta, Iceland's claim to fame in the dessert world. My dad had a migraine, was already cradled in the drugged-up nothingness of sleep.

You know me, I'm not a sweets man, Ari said, *but I make an exception for this. Isn't it beautiful? Layers upon layers upon layers, like it has lived a long life but remains fresh and delicious.*

It was so quiet, just the two of us, without Elizabet's pot-banging and key-jangling and *look-at-me!* screeches. Without Frida skating around in her woollen socks, fussing over me and the baby and Ari. We sat on the floor, on a sheepskin rug that still smelled a little of Elizabet pee. He opened a beer, not my dad's choice, some kind of lager that's almost black. He poured me half into a plastic cup and held up his own. *Here's to warm friends in cold places.*

I wondered if he lay in bed at night dreaming up the things he'd say the next day. He was wearing a plaid flannel shirt, blue and red to match his eyes and lips, and grey long johns. His bare feet were smooth and perfectly sized, with little tufts of strawberry blond hair on top of each one. He cocked his head and smiled at me. *Here's to the woman you will one day be. I wish I would know her.*

What happened next is not entirely clear. All I know is that I began to cry and I'm not a crier. No one in my family is. But there I was, heaving for breath, letting out deep Elizabet-like wails, and then there I was, snotting into Ari's soft, strawberry blond chest, and then his hands were on my cheeks and we were rocking, and then my fingers were in his beard and his tongue was in my mouth.

It's okay, little one. Frida wouldn't mind, you know. We aren't possessive.

I imagined I was Frida and let myself go. My breasts were as round as hers, my skin as clear and rosy. I let myself be comforted, the tears kissed away, let new things happen, come what may. I let myself be Frida, let myself be joyful, just for once, joyful first.

The next day, Mr. Fullham, the principal, passed me in the hallway. "How are you, Jaz? You've made friends with the Icelanders, eh? The wife saw you coming from their place last night. The baby wouldn't sleep so she took him for a drive. It was pretty late."

I don't go back—not to school, and not across the street. At one point, I stand at my bedroom window and watch Ari packing a truck parked out front. He waves, like nothing has happened, his usual jovial, welcoming self. I panic and pull the curtain closed.

Dear Frida: Should I be ashamed?

That was back in April, before any sign of the spring thaw. And nearly a whole summer has passed since Ali and Frida buggered off, but it's like they're preserved in my mind, fresh as ever.

The day my father arrives in town, we go for burgers at VJ's Drive-Inn. Then that afternoon, between the beat-up recycling bins and generous potholes of Gordon's back lane, the Fab Three suddenly find themselves together again for the first time in forever.

My father drops me off just after my mother has arrived. She's standing outside her hybrid hatchback and squinting into the fall sun. Gordon is raking up the first dead leaves in the backyard, the ones that have decided they've had enough, they know what's coming, no use hanging on. I get out and stand awkwardly between the two cars.

"Ready to go?" my mother asks. "Have you eaten?"

To my surprise, my dad gets out, too, stretching as if the economy rental car is too small and he needs to stretch his legs. Gordon stands at attention with the rake.

"Those are some trees," my dad says.

Gordon smiles, as if my dad has just told him he looks better than ever. "Older than the house."

"Have you had lunch, Jaz?" my mother asks.

I try to imagine them as teenagers, the Fab Three, killing time together in the middle of nowhere. But I can't do it. Only they know, these three middle-aged people, and they're not talking.

My dad holds up his hand at my mother, part wave, part message: *settle down*. "We ate. She's like you, no onions on her burger." He looks sad and uncomfortable under the massive, shedding elms.

That night, I don't hear Fen snoring. I can think of Ping only as Fen now because Gordon has said it so many times that it's stuck. *Do you understand, Fen? You must wait for the light. The walking little man, Fen. You must wait for him.*

Fen is crying a quiet *e-soos-me* cry, but it's unmistakable. She is crying.

Dear Frida: Why is Fen crying? Unrequited love? Homesickness? Sore toe?

Dear Frida: I don't think Dad avoids Gordon because he's gay. I think it's because Gordon won, and Dad lost—lost his girls to Gordon, and to the city.

Dear Frida: Once upon a time, there were three star-crossed lovers asleep on ancient rocks. The tide rose up, washed two away, and then there was only one.

As usual, just writing these pointless words makes me feel better.

Blood

Four Facts and a Few Last Words

1. During the height of the North American fur trade, many British and French fur traders married First Nations and Inuit women, and their offspring became known as the Métis. In the mid-nineteenth century, the Red River Métis fought eastern-based Canadian government forces to retain the rights to their traditional trading routes, which led to the government's creation of the Province of Manitoba.

2. Throughout the twentieth century, countless Métis were assimilated into European Canadian populations, making Métis heritage more common than is generally realized. Between 1996 and 2006, however, the population of Canadians who self-identify as Métis nearly doubled, to about 390,000.

3. The Greek word "autós" means self, and the word "autism" was first used by psychiatrist Eugen Bleuler in 1908 to mean morbid self-admiration and withdrawal within self.

4. Temple Grandin, an American autistic and inventor, created the first "hug box"—a metal enclosure that can provide the

comforting pressure and closeness autistic people crave, without the over-stimulation of human contact.

An excerpt from Métis leader Louis Riel's last words before his execution by the Government of Canada: I am no more than you are. I am simply one of the flock, equal to the rest. If it is any satisfaction to the doctor to know what kind of insanity I have, if they are going to call my pretentions insanity, I say, humbly, through the grace of God, I believe I am the prophet of the New World.

In one terrible moment, Marc throws their mother across the room. His sister Monique has just walked in the door from day camp, where a helpful counsellor informed her that she is too fat and that she is Métis.

Their mother sits where she has fallen, leaning against the bookcase filled with Marc's collectors' cards, cradling her elbow, staring at nothing. Marc sits round-shouldered on the bunk bed, rocking a little, and Monique stands frozen in the doorway. It's as if they're afraid to approach their own mother, afraid if they get too close she'll start to wail and wail and never stop.

Monique is fourteen, big for her age but a pixie compared to her thick-chested brother, and the first to speak, as usual. "What the hell?"

Marc strokes his scraggly beard like it's a pet. "Don't come in here."

"What's the matter with you?" Monique asks.

Their mother gets up slowly, straining like she hasn't been to a yoga class in months. "Leave him be."

Monique looks from one to the other. It's dim in Marc's

room, only skinny blades of sun escaping from the roller blind drawn all the way down.

"Leave him be," their mother says again. She's still bent at the waist as if she has PMS cramps. She grabs Monique by the arm and shoves her into the hall. "He's not himself. Just leave him."

"What's going on?" Monique asks.

Their mother opens her lips in what Monique thinks might be a smile, but it's not. She's gritting her teeth. "I said just leave him be."

Marc strokes his beard—purposeful, repetitive, like a cat cleaning itself. Without warning, he flies at the door and slams it with enough force to seal a bank vault. What he would give to find himself in just such a place—dark, silent steel hugging him in from all sides. What he would give to find himself immune to those voices—their mother's softly clinging and relentless, his sister's booming and unpredictable. Each haunts him in its own unique way. Monique's presence is about small oppressions: the way her thighs brush together in jeans, the way she huffs through everyday tasks, the way she chews, her peanut butter breath, her flowery lotions on top of body odour; the way she will appear, huffing, demand something of him he knows not what.

But these are things he has learned to master, by and large. When he was younger, he would stack things, sort his cards, write down the sports stats, backwards and forwards, drown his senses with order of his own making. It is other things, more recent, less easy to pinpoint, to sort and name, that seem to defeat him these days.

There was a time, when he was still a child, that his mother's steady weight on his shoulders could be actually calming. But no longer. Day in, day out, she hovers patiently, gently, suggesting he should shower, and he wants to smash her face in with the amethyst paperweight on his desk. The jagged purple would chew through her pale, tiny-pored skin with just one bite. She has no idea how much the pounding hurts—how the new water-saver showerhead feels like beach pebbles hurling against his skin. How the reek of dandruff shampoo leaves him weak. How her body lotion reminds him of school, of the others brushing past him in the hallway, their exposed arms alarmingly soft, their teeth enamel so white, their toenails painted with tiny, taunting flower designs. They all close in on him and he feels the need to run, to smash through, a bull set loose in the Spanish streets.

He can hear his sister breathing. She is standing behind the closed door, in defiance of their mother. He waits, pets his beard, one hundred strokes, two hundred, but the breathing continues. Does she assume he knows she's there? Monique has never had any idea what he can and cannot do. He opens the door.

"She's in the backyard," she says. "Weeding."

Marc waits. Her breath smells like cheese.

"Did you know we're Métis?" she asks.

"What?"

"Métis," she says. "We have Aboriginal blood."

A few years ago, Marc delved into chemistry, and blood chemistry in particular. Before that, it was astronomy, mapping the constellations with pins on his ceiling, recording both astronomical and, when applicable, mythical identifiers: Corona Australis = centaur shooting arrows; Vulpecula, the fox. Then it was geography, this time drawn in notebooks: Chad bordered by Libya to the north, Sudan to the east, the Central African Republic to the south, Cameroon and Nigeria to the southwest, and Niger to the west. Fiji = 18.1667° S, 178, 4500° E. Then the blood—glucose, potassium, bicarbonate, sodium, creatinine, chloride—only one little ingredient amiss and let's count the ways the body goes into revolt.

"She's from Iceland," he says, as if that's the end of the story. He does not add that Iceland is unique in the world, an isolated, nearly homogeneous population with meticulous genealogical records.

She stares, a long-lashed beef cow trying to decipher genetic code. "I know."

"Okay," he says. "Whatever," and closes the door in her face. He likes this word—*whatever*—says it often, because it is dismissive and also the kind of thing a young man like him might say.

The next day, just after supper, Marc walks out and does not come back. Not that night, or the next one. Their mother heads whole hog into the search, keeping in constant touch with police, making their father drive her around the streets until they both look as stinky and dishevelled as Marc himself.

"He's eighteen, Stef," their father says. "There's only so much we can do." He's rubbing the bridge of his nose where his glasses sit, day in and day out. Monique has a name for this that she's only shared with her friend, Del. It's the *I've been designing motors more complex than your brain all day, leave me the F alone* rub.

Their mother looks at him as if he's retarded, not a big-time engineer and the missing person's dad. "He's special needs, Wayne."

"You're the one who resisted the label," her father says.

Their mother glares, says nothing.

Monique insists Del talk on the phone rather than text—anything to avoid the shitstorm at home.

"I've got more in common with someone in Mongolia than my own brother," Monique says.

It's not a complaint, simply an observation, and one of the things Del loves most about her friend. She is not a whiner.

"Where do you think he is?" Del asks.

Monique hears the counsellor's sing-song voice from the other day chime in from nowhere. *We all have to love our bodies,* which means we need to treat them with love. It's the only one we've got and we've got it for life.

She and Del could talk about that, about how the voice keeps playing like a catchy tune you don't really like, but won't go away. How she could still feel the hand squeezing her shoulder in sisterly assurance: *I'm Métis, too. That's why I do this. I've had diabetes for seven years and my mom lost a leg to the disease. But you still have a chance to change things, to love yourself, to be healthy and strong.*

I do love myself, Monique had wanted to say. I think I deserve everything. I deserve meatball subs, mozzarella sticks, chocolate chip banana bread, garlic toast, burgundy cherry gourmet frozen yoghurt. I deserve it all.

This is something else Del also loves about her. She comes over to Monique's place to escape her highly programmed life—competitive jazz dance, private oboe lessons, tae kwon do, musical theatre. Del's mother is addicted to schedules, has been known to do the treadmill on Christmas day.

"Monnie does her own thing," Del likes to say. "And that is cool."

The truth is, however, Del has no idea what food means to Monique. It's not that Monique doesn't care that her entire wardrobe is made up of large T-shirts and larger yoga pants, or that people call her fat behind her generous back. She does care—just not enough. For as long as she can remember, nothing makes her feel as good, so instantly, obviously, accessibly good, as a snack.

"You're too critical of yourself, Del," Monique likes to say. "You're going to end up in therapy."

This was the kind of stuff they talked about all the time. It was almost a schtick. They'd met when they were eight, on the beach in Grand Marais, where their families both had cabins. Monique's one-room cabin, which sat on a precariously sandy cliff overlooking the shallow lake and her mother called "The

Shack," was a hand-me-down from her father's long-dead paternal grandfather, whereas Del's father had recently purchased a "move-in ready" A-frame nestled in the trees with a new tin roof and vinyl siding. Del is as muscled as Monique is plump. Del is an only child and Monique definitely is not. But they made their pact during a drought summer, when it seemed like the blazing days would go on forever. When heat hung in the night air as if it couldn't bear to let go. When Marc was "coming into his own," as their mother said, becoming an eccentric darling of teachers and able to visit the cabin with minimal "stress-related behavioural incidents." During a sunset made more beautiful by the haze of forest fires to the north, Monique and Del had pledged to be real friends. Not BFFs, not soul sisters, just *real*, no matter what.

Now, Del is confused by her friend's silence. It's not like Monique at all. "Hey-ho," Del says, good and loud into the phone. "You there or what?"

I can help you come up with plan, a weekly menu. It won't be that hard, I promise. Next year, you'll probably be a junior counsellor yourself. Don't you want to pass on healthy habits to the kids? Be a role model? Our people need role models.

Monique is confused. Our people? Did the counsellor mean fatties or the Métis? Did she really think Monique was going to spend her summer, the summer her brother finally went psycho, eating lentils and carrots?

"Mon?"

"Sorry," Monique lies. "Gotta go. My dad's hovering. I'll keep you updated."

This is what Marc knows. He no longer has any control. The old tricks have lost their magic. So he keeps on the move, counting light standards, passing buses, reciting the constellations spelled backwards, in alphabetical order.

He knows people no longer crowd him. Not like when he was younger, when he was quiet and tall and clean, the school novelty with the eerie memory and stubborn mother. They move around now, part the sea, even the ones with suntanned legs bared all the way up to their cracks, moon-like breasts stuffed high, a pair of udders in a bra. So he keeps going, keeps muttering until he has no choice but to collapse in a park, pungent and spent.

When they track him down at the shelter for street youth, he knows what to say. I am of age. I am safe. I choose to be here.

He does not say that he has lost control. That he has stopped stroking his beard and is instead making fists, digging his uncut nails into his palms, waiting exactly five seconds, then repeating.

This is what Monique knows. Her mother's grandparents on both sides came from Iceland. Her mother's father set himself up running a gas station and car dealership in the Interlake.

"Your dad had a hick French accent," her mother liked to say, one of those jokes that Monique never quite got. "But they forgave him because he had a degree and would look after me in the style to which I'd become accustomed."

She knows her father spoke French before English, that he grew up fishing on Lake Winnipeg. She knows his father, Monique's grandfather, died when he was five, his mother when he was at university.

She knows her mother blogs about all of them, but mostly Marc and his autism. She rarely reads the entries because they're usually something like this:

Wayne set up a man-cave for himself where he fixes old cars he can never bring himself to sell. Where is my escape? Perhaps this is it. My daughter, still so young, doesn't seem to need one. She's always here, so affable, so available, as if compensating for her brother's absent presence.

Monique knows she is the easy one. She knows this is not a good time. She knows Del loves her for who she is, blubber and crazy brilliant brother and all, but Del cannot help her with the counsellor's chirp-chirp-chirping voice.

While Monique is lying to her friend for the very first time, Marc counts the steps between garages in an inner-city back lane. The lanes are quieter, darker, simpler, than the streets, and at times, he feels capable of roaming and breathing at the same time. At this hour, not long before sunset, everything—the relentless chain-link fences, the winter-ravaged driveways and sagging garage doors, the sharp thistle emerging through every available crack and crevice—seems to lose its edge.

Marc does not like movies, not the horrific surround sound or rows upon rows of invisible munching mouths, not the in-your-face faces and droning music montages, but one time his father made him sit down at home and watch something called *My Winnipeg*, and Marc watched it again and again. It was as if its crawling images and meandering, undemanding voice spoke to him, and only him, like nothing before. In it were the unmarked back lanes of Winnipeg—snow-grey, moon-lit, fogged with exhaust—and he felt a kind of familiarity utterly new to him.

He was twelve years and three months old the day it hit him that he was a freak when it came to language. Other people did not hear the word *attitude* and see a plaid fedora perched atop a faceless, genderless white mannequin. Or hear the name *Monique* without seeing the enormous, sad-eyed dairy cow, patiently putting up with the milking machine at the dairy farm they'd visited on a school field trip. *Dad* was a '71 Camaro, steel blue, with worn sheepskin seat covers and its hood up. *Peace* was a perfectly round, perfectly pink-frosted birthday cake cut in eight identical-sized pieces. After the movie, *Winnipeg* became their potholed back lane in the depth of January. Only the word *mom* remained imageless, was simply an everyday sound, like *bang* or *pop*.

This summer night, the garbage is a distasteful mix of sweet and sour, but there's a breeze and it doesn't linger. There are no street numbers on the garages, but Marc has counted from both the beginning and end of the block and can recite each address as he passes. He knows he must do this until he's spent, can do it no longer, before returning to the shelter to pass out. Otherwise there might be trouble. He knows this, he can feel it, but cannot explain it. The girls there—*girl = the bodiless doll head Monique once had for playing hair stylist*—came too close with their wrinkled, low-slung skirts and diamond-studded belly buttons.

"It's okay," one had said. "We're all freaks here, sweetie."

And he ran like she'd tried to bite him, because he wanted to take her tiny bird head, covered in blonde hair so thin you could see the sun-burnt scalp beneath, and crush it in his grown-man hands.

134 Gertrude. 137. 138. 141, Marc counts. *Freak* is his word, not hers. From the first time he heard it, on the history channel, during the show about the man long ago who travelled around drawing perfect architectural reproductions of cathedrals after seeing them once, he loved it. He loves the softness of the *f* followed by the *k*'s punch, would repeat it just for fun even when his mother asked him to stop. It didn't matter when he learned the word *savant. Freak = a cathedral* and he can't shake it.

A garage door begins to rumble and Marc nearly buckles to his knees. Brake lights glow angry red in the dying light and he ducks in behind a recycling bin at 147, tries to hide his bulky self as best he can. He watches the gravel give way beneath the tires, counts those that bounce free as the wheels grind and straighten, does not notice the black dog until its nose is directly under his elbow.

Marc straightens, steps away, crushes a soft metal downspout with his rancid runner, stumbles back against a stuccoed garage wall. The pain is immediate and sharp, but he does not cry out. The black dog in the dying light watches him from the middle of the lane, then takes three small steps closer. He sniffs the sweet and sour air and takes two more steps.

Their mother said she first had Marc tested when he was two-and-a-half because he couldn't tell the difference between the neigbour's dog and the neighbour's cat. He remembers watching a show, not long ago, about a three-year-old black standard poodle that could tell when his master was about to have a seizure. The dog could tell maybe thirty minutes before it happened.

Still crumpled against the wall, Marc fishes the half-doughnut from his shirt pocket. They'd handed them out at the shelter, and the crust of sugar covering the trans-fatty goo had been too much for his senses, like grinding chewy sand between his teeth. He holds out the sticky remains in his palm and the dog bounds at him, no holds barred, inhales the doughnut, begins to lick every last grain of goodness from the generous stranger's hand. Marc lets him, almost likes the wet, rough tongue appealing to his skin for more, more, more. The dog pauses, waits, shoves his muzzle into Marc's broad chest, nestles there, sniffs, breathes, pauses. Somewhere, a door slams and the black dog runs, disappears into the dying light.

Marc almost wishes he'd had more squished doughnut to offer, almost wishes the dog, with its hot saliva and opaque eyes, had stayed with him longer (*forever* = ∞).

"Twenty-seven," he says aloud. Twenty-seven bits of gravel went flying beneath the wheel.

Her brother has not been home for five nights when Monique approaches their mother. It's fairly late, past eleven, and she's buoyed by a recent sub sandwich trip. Her mother is fresh from a long bath, and with her wet hair combed back her eyes look squinty, as if the hot water hasn't just wrinkled her fingers and toes but turned all of her into an old lady. She slathers cream over her face as Monique comes up from behind, flops on the unmade king-sized bed. "So is Dad Métis?"

"Hmmm?"

"Dad. Is he Métis?"

Her mother studies herself and sighs, starts dousing cream on her neck. "Depends. His grandmother was Cree, I think. So I suppose that would qualify. You'd have to ask him."

Monique absently tugs at a loose thread on the quilt, wonders whether, if she pulled and pulled, the whole thing would come apart. "Why don't you know? Shouldn't we know?"

Her mother sighs again, tosses the lotion aside, and lies down beside Monique, the way they used to do sometimes. It started the year Monique was ten and got her period and Marc was elected president of the chemistry club. "What are you going on about, hon? She died a long time ago, when Dad's mom was a baby. He never knew her."

"Okay, but the name. Traverse? It's Métis?"

Her mother hooks her pinkie into Monique's and gives it a tug, like she used to do sometimes. "Yeah, I suppose. Yeah."

But it wasn't like it used to be. She sounded so tired, so old, that Monique didn't have the heart to take it further. Not the Métis thing, and certainly not the weight thing. Even though her mother has warned her of the "personal nature" of her blog, Monique can't resist taking a peek now and then.

I fear the youngest, my so-called normal child, has paid a price for her brother's journey into our world. Our Monique was always so healthy, so hardy, I hardly noticed when she literally began bursting at the seams, as if by taking up more physical space she might get her due. That third glass of chocolate milk, that second croissant, that bag of butterscotch chips in the back of the fridge, it was all so easy to provide, so natural, in a household where every day was a fight for her brother's retreating mind.

So she tracks down her father in the garage workshop. Years ago, he'd set it up to be Marc-friendly—no fluorescent lighting, no fans, nothing flashy or loud or smelly—and the two of them had spent hours upon hours out there.

"Leave the boys be," her mother would say. "They're tinkering." Those were good days, the period between Marc's tantrums and his obsession with sports cards.

The overhead door is open and Monique patters in her slippers across the immaculate concrete floor. Her father is pouring something into the engine of a red antique farm truck.

"Dad," she says.

He starts and the liquid, probably oil, misses its mark for just a moment. He doesn't speak until he's finished the job, thrown the empty bottle in the recycling bin, wiped his hands, and settled down on the green camping chair where he drinks his daily Scotch on the rocks. "Jesus, Mon. You scared me."

Monique tightens the belt around her terry towel robe, as if suddenly shy. "Sorry."

He shoves his thumb and forefinger beneath his glasses and does the rub. He's wearing a white work T-shirt that's been washed too many times, and when he slouches back in the chair his stomach bulges a little over his belt. This is new.

"I was just wondering," Monique says, suddenly feeling like a giant standing over him in the low chair, "why we never talk about being Métis."

He shrugs, as if he's been expecting the question. "No reason. It's just not my thing, Mon. I barely remember my mom and it was her side that was Ojibway."

"Mom said Cree."

He shrugs again. "Cree, Ojibway, they all occupied the same space."

"But shouldn't you be proud of your Métis heritage?" Monique asks. The counsellor's voice was so clear, so confident, so caring. It's like he was missing the point. "They need role models."

Her father laughs and kicks her knee playfully with his runner. "I'm no more Métis than anyone else around here. That's not my thing, Mon. But you go for it. Be proud. Fly the flag."

It's good to see him laugh, but she will not let herself be deterred. "Did diabetes run in your family?"

He scratches his chin, acts like he is finally paying attention. "Well, my parents died young of other causes, so it wasn't much of an issue. But probably. That's why I worry about you."

"You worry? You never say anything."

He sits up, tugs at the belt of her robe. "That doesn't mean I don't worry."

What good is it if I don't know? Monique wants to ask.

But her father has removed his glasses completely and the time for real questions is probably over.

"You're still growing," he says. "The doc says it may all even out in the end. Okay, Mon? You're good. You're great."

Monique makes a couple of body builder poses, and then turns away before he can see her cry. It strikes her for the first time, at fourteen years old, that the world is a frightening place. Marc has always seemed to know that, spending most of their childhood hollering in fear and rage over things no one else seemed to notice. It was the small things that made him crazy, but never the big ones—the ones you had no idea even existed until you grew older and it all got complicated.

Outside the garage, Monique kneels down on her father's meticulous grass. She'd read once in the blog: *Many autistics will not see a regular suburban back yard and think "there is a lawn," but instead, they will see each individual blade of grass. Imagine.*

Could it be that her brother's brilliance lay not in his weird talents, but his ability to avoid wading into real life? To avoid his screwed-up self, his screwed-up family, this screwed-up world?

She was alone, on the blades, beneath the suburban stars,

and there was no one to ask, to check in with—not Del, not her parents, and certainly not her brother. Marc had buggered off, deserted her here, alone with her strangely silent grown-up tears.

Marc walks along the gravel shoulder of Highway 6, before the turn-off to Grand Beach. Long-weekend traffic roars by and he almost welcomes the whiz of their breeze. He can feel the back of his neck burning, feel his underpants sopping wet against him. He is not suited to being on the run, he knows this, but he soldiers on, one foot in front of the other, heading to The Shack like a homing pigeon. He is too hot to count, too tired to panic. He barely notices when a vehicle eases onto the shoulder, rumbles up beside him. A hand reaches out but doesn't touch.

"Marc. Marc, honey." It's a women's voice, but not *the* voice, not the three-letter word with no image to give it shape—*mom*.

She is practically hanging out the window now. "It's Marlene. Marlene Knight. What you doing, hon? You going to the cabin? You need a ride?"

It's the red Subaru 4X4 from down the road, near the chip stand. Before that, they drove a red Honda hatchback. She asks questions so quickly it's like she doesn't expect answers.

"Marc, hon? You look a sight, honey. Do you have water? We've got water here. Chris and I are heading right your way. Climb in. We'll give you a lift."

Marc walks on, lets the sweat drip into his eyes, waits for them to grow as tired as he is.

"Do your folks know you're here? Do you want me to call them? I have their number somewhere."

"I'm of age," Marc says. "I'm eighteen."

"Marlene, take it easy." It's a male voice, the driver who likes red. "Let him be. It's not far."

They drive along beside him for thirty-four seconds more,

then are gone. He has no more sense of time, no sense of his body moving through space until he is submerged in water.

The shallow lake, the tenth largest in the world, has always been abnormally warm for a fresh body of water, but the brownish film is more recent.

For centuries, his father told him, the sandy bottom has taken down fishers in the mildest of storms. "It doesn't take much to stir this pot. Twice, my own father, your grandfather, nearly died beneath the whitecaps, but then he lived to drown in his own bathtub when his heart gave out. One of the perils of living alone, I guess."

Marc has read that due to run-off of agricultural fertilizers and pesticides, nitrogen and phosphorus levels in the lake have climbed steadily in the last several decades, and algae blooms have skyrocketed. Floating now, he cannot see his fingers beneath the sediment. Some scientists say it's probably too late to save the lake—the chemical, physical, and biological parameters of the water have shifted past the point of no return.

When Monique gets the phone call from Marlene, her father has just taken off for a meeting in Chicago and her mother is at the spa getting *the works*.

"She desperately needs respite," her father had said before he left. "Just one day to herself."

Monique ponders her next step, then calls Del, whose family is heading to the cabin for the weekend. She makes up a strategic, premeditated, grown-up lie for the first time in her life. She tells Del and her parents that her own mother is already at Grand Beach, her father is delayed, and supper will be waiting. The whole way there in the backseat with her friend, Monique plays gin rummy and makes the usual conversation, amazed at how easily more lies come.

When they drop her off, The Shack shows no sign of life.

Monique immediately makes her way down the gravel road, onto the path obscured by tall grass, and through the willow bush to the rocky cove they used to treat like their own private hideaway. As kids, they called it Ladybug Beach for no particular reason. If anything, it's a haven for mosquitoes and teenagers looking for a place to drink. But it was the only place Marc would put even a toe in the lake.

Monique kicks off her sandals as she sinks into the powdery sand. She's an expert at avoiding the small sticks and stones that can puncture your bare soles and send you howling. At the foamy shore, she contemplates taking off her sweaty T-shirt and size 16 nylon skort, then wades right in, as Marc did, clothes be damned.

He's floating with his eyes closed, disgustingly worn-out runners still on, poking out of the water like beach litter. The water is still only at Monique's waist, so she crouches down, immerses herself completely, then returns puffing to the air. She leans back alongside her brother, lets herself become light, just like that. For the first time, she waits, without a word.

"The one with the crooked teeth and the black dog," Marc says, "she kept getting close, I don't know why, she was out of her head and so I threw her, and she flew." He laughs, not ha-ha, but can you believe it? "She flew."

Monique closes her eyes. She hasn't eaten since breakfast, and her stomach is growling pathetically, like a toy poodle.

"I don't know what's going to happen," Marc says.

"It's okay, Marc," she says. "It's okay not to know. It's okay."

And for one happy moment, Marc and Monique float in the shallow lake, side-by-side, light and cool, their fingers touching now and then by accident. Nothing matters, not Métis blood, or blood sugar. Not the distant constellations or the dying lake. They are floating side-by-side and that's enough.

Roma Raj

Five Facts

1. More than a million Asian Indians are millionaires, but most live on less than $2 per day. An estimated 35% of India's population lives below the poverty line.
2. The absence of a written history has meant that the origin of the Romani people has long been a mystery. But recent genetic studies suggest that Roma gypsies are descended from low-caste "untouchables" who migrated from the Indian sub-continent 1,400 years ago.
3. India has the world's largest movie industry, based in the city of Mumbai (known as the City of Dreams). Almost all "Bollywood" movies are musicals.
4. Romani children are traditionally allowed limited access to non-Romani culture as a way to protect them from outside influence. In the past, Romani gypsies typically married between the ages of nine and fourteen. Today, Romani youth tend to marry in their late teens.
5. Arranged marriage, which is still widely practised in India,

is no longer the norm among Canadian-born Indians. However, marriages are sometimes still arranged by parents within their specific caste or Indian ethnic community.

Since it may be difficult to find someone of the same Indian ethnic background with the desired characteristics, some Indo-Canadians now opt to use a "matchmaker" or online services to find a marriage partner.

Jagat, I saw the way you looked at that girl. The one sitting on the curb as we came out of the clinic, with the mammoth black mutt who surely outweighed her, and the sign written with girlishly round letters on cardboard ripped from a detergent box: "Dog and I both in need of kibble. Please give what you can."

I fish in my pockets, into the jangle of change I know you make fun of, toss a few loonies in her overturned fedora. You can't believe, never expected your old man with his European sandals and expensive watch to do such a thing. I know you want to say something, express your surprise, but you don't, because you think I don't have much to tell you anymore. You've won your scholarships, you've proven yourself, you're ready to walk away and make your mark.

You would never guess that I was trembling as I threw those coins. What kind of son your age would notice such things about his father? You were too busy gazing down the front of her blouse, perhaps experiencing a more-common-than-you'd-think mix of pity and desire. If I began telling you the story of Gypsy Joan, you'd be quickly bored and think you know how it ends. But again your old man might surprise you.

Perhaps I'm being presumptuous. At times, your mother has accused me of assuming the world revolves around Raj, whatever that means. You're probably preoccupied with your own thoughts, your own precarious health, your own gleaming future, didn't even notice I'd tossed the coins. Your mother, who is probably the better parent, would be preoccupied with you too, would not resent, deep down, having to take you to your oncologist uncle who has hospital wings named after him and thinks his shit doesn't stink.

"He's young, in tip-top shape," I said to your mother. "Why assume the worst?"

She looked at me as if I was suggesting we sit and eat chutney as the house burns down around us. "You don't mess around with lumps, Raj. You know that."

She meant I, as a medical professional, should know that. Although I'm sure, though he has never said it, my brother does not consider optometrists part of the holy brethren of doctors.

"Who knows how long it's been there," she pointed out. "He was probably embarrassed to bring it up."

A pea-sized lump on your upper leg, just below the right testicle—almost certainly fatty build-up. But this morning, your uncle, ever the conquering hero, sent it out for biopsy "just to be safe."

When was the last time we walked through a downtown street as father and son? Years perhaps, not since I moved the office to St. James, where the rent is cheaper and the parking free. You walk alongside me, practically a grown man, and show no sign of worry or concern over your fate. You notice the parking ticket before I do, slide it out from beneath the windshield wiper as if retrieving an anonymous love letter.

"Bastards," you say, in mock rage. You've taken to cursing in front of your old man to see how I'll react, but I refuse to give you any satisfaction.

My brother had kept us waiting for thirty-five minutes, claiming an early morning emergency at the hospital.

"I told you to buy an extra half hour," you say. "Uncle's always overbooked."

I don't point out that I've left my own practice for the entire morning because your mother insisted I accompany you.

"If I could go, I would," she said, "but you know I already promised Sonja." I have no idea what she promised Sonja, but it takes so much energy to argue sometimes. I assume you would've preferred to meet with your uncle alone, but as you'll learn, we have to pick our battles, son.

My golf jacket from last night sits rumpled into a ball between our seats and you struggle a moment with your seat belt before shoving the jacket testily into the back. It's not that long ago that I struggled with the belts of your car seat, yanking off my gloves with my teeth, swearing under my breath in the deep freeze, testily making sure you were as safe as humanly possible.

I steal a glance at your handsome face, all dark lashes and full lips, the kind women become fools over.

You stare blankly, unreadable. A true lady-killer, like your uncle. "What?"

"Nothing," I say. "I'm not allowed to look at you?"

The next morning, your two sisters are still sleeping but your sneakers are already on. You've made yourself something called a smoothie, and I know you'd mock me for calling your footwear the wrong thing. *Trainers*—you're already up, in your *trainers*, not one to let summer vacation slow you down. You're such a hard worker, so single-minded in your goals, I don't know what I did to breed such an achiever. It's as if all I had to do was not stand in your way, and yet now, on this flawless summer morning, I want to stop you and make you listen.

I was older than you, I'd say, already engaged to your mother, in fact, when I met her. She hung around the campus, literally, not a student but a hanger-on, bumming food and cigarettes from those whose parents were footing their tuition bills. I was aware of her for some time, but without ever actually encountering her. She was widely known as "Gypsy Joan," because of her flowing skirts and untidy hair, and because she asked people to call her that. She was fair, though, pale blue eyes like robin's eggs, hair as yellow as that of a cartoon princess. She was what you might call a fixture on the scene, a point of interest, someone who did not belong but who was always there. I rarely gave her a second thought.

But all that changed one late spring afternoon, when the last of the snow was finally giving up the ghost. I know, I know, it sounds like a cliché that it happened in April, but some things only become trite because they are common. I had just finished an English exam, my worst subject, which you might find surprising, since I'm such a reader now. But my brothers and I had been groomed for the sciences and it was a fine line to study the novels just enough to get top marks, but not so much that they'd take away from what really mattered.

I'd written my second essay on *Crime and Punishment* and was crossing the lawn between Fletcher Argue Hall and the student commons, checking if I'd spelled the protagonist's name correctly (no: it is Raskolnikov, not Raskalov), when I nearly tripped over her feet. She'd kicked off her shoes and was lying amongst the still-bare charcoal trees, on her back on the brown grass in only a light cotton dress, twirling a cigarette in her sticklike fingers.

I apologized, though I had no reason to. She was lying directly in a shortcut frequented by students late for class.

"Do you have a light?" she asked.

I feigned ongoing absorption in my Russian book, kept on walking. "Don't smoke."

"Wait!" she called.

Now, I have no idea to this day why I turned back to her. I had an inkling that young men spoke of her as an easy conquest, a free spirit who wasn't above trading on her obvious appeals. I knew your mother would be transferring to this very campus in the fall and had no interest in her hearing any lurid rumours when it came to her future husband. Maybe it was the Russians. Or the spring cliché. Or perhaps it had always been in me, this turning back despite myself.

She bent her knees, did a sit-up and folded in on herself. I suppose anything's possible in a loose cotton dress. "What's your name?"

The sun was in my eyes, but I spoke to the small ball of girl on the grass. "Raj."

She laughed, ear still resting on her bony knee. "Of course it is. You look like a Raj."

I had no clue what she meant by this, other than I was Indian and I had a stereotypical Indian name. Even then, I was a little pudgy and was known to slouch beneath my backpack, so there was absolutely nothing regal about my bearing.

"Straighten up, for goodness' sake," your mother would say to me in those days. "With that long neck you'll end up looking like a turtle by middle age."

And it's true, your mother's reminders have kept me from such a fate. Today, I have better posture than many men half my age.

I tucked the novel in my jacket pocket and utterly surprised myself by saying: "And yours?"

Bathed in backlight, she kicked her legs out straight, and though I could barely see her eyes, I could make out tiny blonde hairs shining on her deathly pale skin. "My name?"

"Yes," I said.

"Don't you know it?"

She was good at this, reeling you in and throwing you off.

"Yes, I suppose."

"Then why did you ask?"

I shrugged, maybe for the first time in my life. My mother thought it a disrespectful gesture. "To be polite," I said.

She laughed again, high and girlish, slightly forced. "That's lovely. I like that, Raj. Just being polite."

I know now that I am never a half-hog person. I only go whole-hog, as they say. What else can explain what I did next? "I just finished my most unpleasant exam. Would you like some tea, or something?"

She stood then, took two steps towards me, out of the sunlight and into the shade of a mighty old elm trunk, and it's then I really noticed the robin's egg eyes and princess hair. "Really? Just to celebrate? That's lovely. You're lovely, Raj."

"Raj. It's 8:20. What are you doing there?"

Your mother is downstairs now, looking rounder but still beautiful in her burnt orange pantsuit. I tease her that she shops at the Health Care Administrator Fashion Outlet.

"Yes, yes," I say, making no move to get up from the table. "I'm hazy this morning. Can't seem to get going."

She grabs a breakfast bar, pours coffee into a thermos mug. Your older sister got me one for Christmas but I don't dare tell her that it works too well and I've burnt my tongue numerous times.

"Should he be out there running?" she asks, "before we know what's going on?"

But she's practically out the door before I can answer, seems content to plant a seed of worry and bugger off.

"You know you're being irrational," I yell after her. "You'll make the boy anxious for nothing."

You're still gone when I must leave or miss my first appointment. It's the grandchild of an acquaintance, who has never been quizzed while staring through a beastly metal head, and I'll have to be my charming best.

But one more thing before I go, because you'll scarcely believe it of your father. As we walked towards the cafeteria, Gypsy Joan and I, it became clear that the back of her cotton dress was soaked through, a victim of early spring melt, and so

I draped my jacket over her shoulders. She hugged it tight, as if afraid it might run away, and laughed. "You are lovely, Raj. Truly and really lovely."

It was as if no one had ever offered to buy her tea before.

"The lab call?" you ask.

You wake me from a nap and I start with a shuddering *huff*, just like my father used to. I'd been dreaming of the girl with the mutt and the kibble sign. "A few coins," she'd said to me. "Aren't you rich now, Raj?" It's not hard to see what my subconscious is doing. I've gone through periods where I dream of Gypsy Joan often, but don't make too much of it. I also dream of your mother's younger sister in Toronto.

I put on my glasses, check the time as if it's relevant—shortly after eight in the evening. Two days since we visited your uncle. "Not yet," I say. "But don't sweat it. If it was something serious, they'd call ASAP."

"I know," you say, already turning away, as if I've insulted you. "I just asked."

Hold on, I want to say. Or maybe *freeze, mister*, like your mother and I used to say when we meant business. But you're not reaching for the sharp knife your mother has set aside after chopping coriander. You're simply turning away from me.

Why would you care about your old man's lusty reminiscences? But that was not all, not by a long shot. That afternoon, over tea, Gypsy Joan and I talked for three hours and I was late for your grandmother's hallowed supper hour.

"So Raj, are you Hindu? she asked. "Do you worship cows, and little elephant statues, and dream of bathing in the polluted Ganges?"

For some reason, I was not offended in the least. Perhaps it was the way she said it, with such energy and enthusiasm—her legs were crossed and her tiny foot bounced the whole time, as if keeping rhythm to some inner beat. She acted as if meeting a real Hindu would be the highlight of her month.

I smiled indulgently. "I'm not terribly religious. My family has always been great believers in a democratic, secular India."

She nodded solemnly, and I was instantly sorry. It's true, I can make your mother laugh by doing an excellent imitation of her father, but I've never been particularly good at keeping things light and fun. Gypsy Joan's pale face did not suit solemnity.

"Still," I said, "after death, I'm hoping to come back as rich lady's lapdog."

She clapped her hands and laughed and the pinky hue returned to her cheeks. It was enough to spur me on. "What about you? What's with the name? Where did it come from?"

She leaned forward as if imparting a great and eternal secret. "Well, I'm a gypsy and my name is Joan, so there you have it."

"But surely you're not gypsy," I said. "You look classically Nordic. Swedish, maybe, or Icelandic."

She wagged her finger at me. "Aah, don't be so narrow-minded. I'm a gypsy by choice and surely that counts for something."

Her small breasts were bare beneath the thin cotton and I tried to keep my eyes on her bony hands cradling the teacup. For some reason, I had a hard time looking into those eyes, as if I might disappear into their blue horizon.

But I know what you're thinking. By the time you were twelve, you'd seen plenty of gypsies in the streets of Europe—family vacation stops in Paris, Venice, Rome while on our way to the South Asian seas. It had troubled you, Jagat, for quite some time to see the filthy children peeing on the cobblestones, the bent-over old women moaning in the streets, begging in foreign tongues. Your brand new point-and-shoot camera was plucked right from your jacket pocket by a little gypsy girl pretending to let you pet her mangy cat.

"Why are they like that, Papa?" you asked me. "What's the matter with them?"

I bought you another camera, tried to brush off your questions as best I could. "It's the way they've always lived," I said. "Some things are very difficult to change."

I didn't bother lecturing you the way I did that poor perky-nippled young girl over afternoon tea. In our family, if you knew something special, it was meant to be shared, your listener imparted with whatever wisdom you had to offer. And I just so happened to know a little something about gypsies, since my sister had recently written a history paper on migration in Eastern Europe.

Actually, the gypsies now like to be referred to as Roma, I told her. We now know they emigrated from India well over a thousand years ago, probably members of a low caste with few opportunities. I also mentioned that the Roma culture was profoundly patriarchal, with young girls known to marry before their fourteenth birthdays.

She took a bite of my half-eaten apple cruller, and then shoved the rest against my moving lips.

"Okay, yes," she interrupted. "They also go where they want, when they want, and they don't give two shits what you think of them."

I took hold of her hand to push it away, but instead, I too took a bite of pastry. Then she fed me another, and another, until my mouth was surrounded by a ring of sticky sugar which she brushed away with her pale, bony hand.

Then she sucked on her index finger and gazed at me. "Roma Raj," she said. "That's what we'll call you. Introducing The Lovely Roma Raj."

Your mother fusses over you to deflect her worry, preparing your favourite meals, buying you the overpriced *trainers* you had your eye on, while she takes out her anxiety on me.

"It's been four days," she says. "Call Mehta. Ask him how long it usually takes."

"I refuse to get worked up over this," I say. "If it was serious, we'd know, and since it's not, we can wait."

"He's your brother," she says. "Just call him."

Perhaps she senses my betrayal, senses I'm somewhere else where she has no business. Over the course of our whole marriage I've never indulged in such extramarital musings except in dreams, and now, when our only son, our shining star, is in mortal peril, I'm adrift. But you see, Jagat, it's not that I don't care. It's that I can't seem to shake this thing I must share with you, somehow, somewhere.

I go over how things played out while soaping up my chest in the shower. Gypsy Joan said she was looking after an apartment for a sessional lecturer, a big old tumbledown beauty by the legislative building. I have no idea what the real story was, but that's where we went. I can count on two hands the number of times she led me up the ample marble stairs, down those wide hallways that reminded her of a bowling alley, and into her "flat," as she called it, like the British, with its useless fireplace mantel and wall sconces in the shape of Victorian candles. But I can still hear the distinct marble echo of those hallways, smell the mix of decaying wood and other people's dinners. There was something melancholy about the place, at one time its central location catering to up-and-coming politicians, lawyers, doctors, and now offering cheap rent for down-on-their luck sessional lecturers clamouring for the few tenure-track positions available.

"Isn't it grand?" she asked. "She's away until June and it's all mine until then."

I felt ashamed I'd assumed the place belonged to a *he*. "Then what?" I asked. "Where do you usually live?"

She flopped down on an uncomfortable-looking futon and kicked her feet into the air. Her knees were as bony as Pippi Longstocking's, the tiny Swedish heroine as strong as an ox I used to watch on Saturday mornings. Do you know Pippi, Jagat? No, of course you don't. She was only a child but lived by herself in a colourful old mansion with a spotted horse named Old Man and a monkey named Sir Nielson, eating all the candy she wanted, engaging in crazy adventures, and saving the day with her feats of daring and strength while her papa sailed the seven seas.

"Here and there," Gypsy Joan said. That night, the spring weather had gone on hiatus and it was chilly beneath the high ceilings. Her nipples stood at attention beneath the cotton dress. "I always find something."

I'm not sure how experienced you are, son. They say your generation begins so young, but when would a boy like you have time? You seem absorbed by your track and your basketball and your science projects and your computer games where you build worlds. I too was innocent even for my time. I came from a more traditional culture. You've never asked, but your sisters have, they go on about it, about how your mother's and my marriage was arranged by our families. We had a say, of course, we could decide if we liked each other, if it seemed to suit us; our families were educated people, after all. But I was innocent physically, and Gypsy Joan and I did not go to bed until the last time we met, after I'd had time to fall in love.

I know it sounds ludicrous, but I can assure you it's true. She did not drink, but she smoked pot, and for hours upon hours, while she toked and I ate microwave popcorn out of the bag, we talked of haphazard things and I fell in love with the dancer's arch of her pale, bouncing foot, the way her brow knitted together when she was thoughtful, a habit that would surely leave lines in her blonde girl forehead by the time she was middle-aged. But I loved even the thought of that, for she seemed so eager to drink in all I said, so full of piss and vinegar and Pippi-like fun, that it was as if she became ageless for me—a gap-toothed urchin, an alluring young filly, a wizened old woman.

I talked of India, of its ancient, festering castes and its lumbering populace potential; I talked of student politics, how they were so petty and yet so necessary; I even talked of your mother, her perfect nostrils honoured with a tiny diamond, her self-assurance, her deep belly laugh, so hard-won but so worth it. She told me stories of the characters she'd met: Kevin the chemistry major who was afraid of armpit hair; Jan the caretaker who had all the makings of a serial killer; Christy the street kid who'd escaped her lecherous stepfather only to take up with a lecherous youth counsellor.

For the first time in my life, I half-believed in karma. I told her of the Roma woman I saw in Florence when I was maybe fifteen. She approached the sun-stroked, sweat-soaked line I was standing in for some museum or another and seemed about to thrust the snot-faced, snivelling infant she held into another woman's arms. As the victim instinctively reached to catch the bundle, the gyspy reached expertly into the woman's purse. I saw the whole thing, saw the gypsy mother's dark, impassive face as she mumbled incomprehensibly, saw her remain just as inscrutable as she got her prize. From my position in line, I had a perfect view of the entire transaction, and when she locked eyes with me, the gypsy with her snotty bait, she knew I knew and yet made no effort to hurry away. She stared haughtily, as if daring me to make a peep, and I made no sound, did not give her away. From then on, it's as if I held our guilt in my pocket, a sharp shard of slate, black as her eyes, that I could cut myself on whenever the mood came over me.

Gypsy Joan clapped her hands in glee. "See, you really are Roma, Raj. You've always sensed that all possession is theft.

Together, we'll travel the world, robbing from stupid, bus-tour Americans and eating carved meat from street vendors."

Part of me really did believe it was karma that it finally happened, after hours upon hours of heavy talking. It began with her sucking the popcorn salt from my fingers and went from there, as natural as our conversation, the two of us on that rock-hard futon, laughing and fumbling and then surprisingly intense. Still, I would spare you the details, a son's embarrassment and possibly disgust, save such things for my old-man dreams.

"Raj, are you still in there? You take longer than the girls, for goodness' sake."

Your mother is knocking on the bathroom door. I don't dignify this with an answer. She knows I am still showering.

"We have to take him back. The results were inconclusive, whatever that means."

"I'll take him," I shout.

"No, I've got nothing until after lunch. I can go."

Her tone of voice means there is no arguing. She wants to speak with Mehta herself, ensure nothing like this happens again.

But sometime soon, I will share the heartache, Jagat, the hollow, physical ache, of when she disappeared. After three more nights of lovemaking, I arrived to find no one but a jet-lagged sessional lecturer peering at me suspiciously through the peephole.

"I came back early. I don't know where she is. I think she goes to the shelter sometimes."

I had no idea what shelter she might have been referring to, and my pride was badly bruised. I went into the lane behind the apartment, where a giant bin overflowed with burst garbage bags that occupants had sent down the chute attached to their fire escape and Gypsy Joan had gleefully dubbed The Esophagus, and vomited like a street drunk. I had risked everything for her, had opened my heart, shared my triumphs and my guilt, and she had simply left.

I waited. I wandered. But after maybe three weeks, the hollow ache hardened into dull, pulsing anger, at her, and at myself. My love had been on the pill and so I had not used protection, god knows why. Perhaps it would've made the whole thing seem premeditated rather than predestined. But the AIDS crisis was at its height and I lived in fear of infection, of having to tell your mother of my transgressions. To this day she does not know that I delayed our wedding by six months not because the hall was double-booked, but because I was anxiously awaiting test results that would put me in the clear.

"Raj, darling, what are you doing? You'll be late. It's 8:20."

I shut the water off, reach for the towel. For months after Gypsy Joan left me, I never felt truly clean. "Yes," I shout through the door. "Yes, I know."

The next day, the phone call comes. The lump is nothing, or whatever it is, it means nothing, and will most likely disappear on its own. I pat you on the shoulder the way a father does, kiss your thick, lady-killer hair.

"I wasn't worried," you say, grinning at me slyly. "Were you?"

"No," I say. "No. But it's different when you're a parent. Some small part of me always worries. Your mother's the same. A more calm and intelligent woman you'll never meet, except when it comes to her children."

She crosses her arms, pretends to be insulted, but her face is pure joy.

You stride across the kitchen in your running shorts and bare chest, the world your oyster. You are leanly muscular, a grown man, but there's something about your state of undress that reminds me of when you were still toddling, still reaching for my knees with your pudgy little paws.

Perhaps you didn't even notice that I threw a few coins in that girl's fedora as we walked from my brother's office. Perhaps you had no idea that I was trembling, never mind needing to know why. You seem such a profoundly driven and disciplined young man. Perhaps you're not prone to my particular weaknesses. And yet I still can't help feeling that you of all people might need to hear my story.

You see, most people would assume that because of this youthful love of mine, I am, deep down, an unhappy man—that I'm someone who still longs for the passion and the freedom I once knew, no matter how briefly, and can never have again. But they would be wrong.

Over the years, I've come to see my first love as the silly and affected young thing that she'd first been from afar. Because you see stereotypes, too, aren't necessarily untruths, and it's like this young woman used them as her yardstick. What would a wild child who sponged off idealistic students be like? She had made an art, or at least a con art, of being Gypsy Joan. And the thing is, much to my sorrow, this has only made me love her more. All those hours of heavy conversation and not once did I try to understand her. Where was her family? What frightened her? How wounded must one be to choose the world's most persecuted, the most despised, the most hopelessly lost people as your guide? How deluded?

Gypsy Joan was lost, and not just to me. She was a lost soul and I doubt she ever found what she was looking for. I live with this painful knowledge every day, Jagat.

Then again, perhaps this is an old man's story, or at least of a man who is no longer young. I look at you standing tall there by your still-beautiful, beaming mother. You're eager to get out there, race the lanes of our leafy neighbourhood—so fit, so alert, so ready—and I have a feeling you wouldn't believe me anyway.

Sandwich Artists

Five Facts

1. Red hair is still honoured amongst Moslems, as the Prophet Mohammed himself was reported to have red hair.
2. Iran is home to one of the world's oldest continuous major civilizations, with historical and urban settlements dating back to 4000 BCE.
3. In the last decade, Iranian-Canadian women have dominated Canada's national beauty pageant circuit.
4. The word "paradise" comes from the Persian for "enclosed garden."
5. In September 2011, Cryos International, one of the world's largest sperm banks, announced that it would no longer accept donations from red-haired men due to low demand from women seeking artificial insemination.

The minute they see each other, they think the same thing: *UGH.*

Casey has been on the job for six shifts and is getting the hang of grabbing just the right fistful of lettuce, not too much so it spills out the side, not too little so they don't think you're being stingy with the rabbit food. Kye is giving Dorri her first-day tour.

"This is the drink machine," he says. "Just push the button—small, medium, large, extra large—and it does all the rest."

He says this as if he's showing her the space arm. Kye is easily impressed, acts as if being assistant manager at a subway sandwich counter inside a hardware outlet doesn't make him a sad case. The place isn't what you'd call busy, more like half-hungry customers trickle in after loading up on drywall or fake designer lamps, but even if it was hopping, he would still be a sad case.

Casey only knows Dorri as *Scarf-face*, a name his friend Rowan came up with. He watches her follow Kye around with the same smug, disinterested expression she has in the hallways at school. She pretends she has no idea who Casey is, and for all he knows, maybe she doesn't. He's always been a blend-in kind of guy.

"Of course, when working with food, we like hairnets," Kye says, as if it was a given that everybody likes hairnets. "But I guess you've got yours built in there, so you're good."

Dorri fakes a smile. She does recognize Casey. She also recognizes that this is their supervisor's, or whatever he is, pathetic attempt at levity. His nervous energy is grating, a radio turned up to eleven and caught between two stations. His chewed fingernails leave her wondering where he spits them.

"Yup," she says, patting her headscarf like it's been a good boy. "I'm always prepared."

Before he leaves for the night, Kye delivers his words of wisdom. He goes over the close routine three times, managing to be both incoherently fast and long-winded. Dorri stops listening halfway through round number two. Kye tells her he's leaving her in Casey's capable hands, as if Casey's been there six years instead of six shifts.

"Friday nights usually mean it's steady," Kye says. "But not in July. Too many cottagers."

Finally, he throws an enormous empty-looking backpack over his shoulder, waves wistfully as an explorer leaving his mates behind on a deserted island. "Good luck, kids."

Dorri crosses her arms, takes a deep breath, tries to remain calm. "What an asshole."

Kye is barely out of earshot. By the look on her face at school, Casey had assumed she was an uptight religious bitch, but it turns out she was just a bitch-bitch. He waits until Kye is safely outside, gliding past the window on his twinkletoes. Kye walks like his heels are too delicate to hit the pavement so he has to glide along on the balls of his feet. Together, they watch him stumble over a discarded pack of gum, watch him give them the thumbs-up sign.

"I don't know," Casey says. "More like a moron."

Dorri doesn't respond. It has begun to sink in that this is perhaps the last place on earth she would choose to spend a summer's night; that it's possible the smell of processed sandwich meat will seep into her pores until dogs start following her home; that she's stuck in an over-air-conditioned, underlit counter cage with a nearly grown man named Casey.

The year before, it had gotten out that he was named after one of the puppets on an old kids' show called *Mr. Dressup*. This was the kind of information that, no matter how friendless you were in class, you couldn't help finding out about. That was how it worked: school forced you to share precious brain space with people and subjects not of your own choosing.

One day, every member of the student body just knew Casey's mother was the school secretary and had spilled the beans about how she'd named her only son after a doggy puppet. The next day, despite yourself, you were taking note of him in the hall: a pudgy body on a skinny frame, pimples on the neck, light reddish hair that would probably fall out early. Casey the puppet:

affable, geeky, forgettable, and his friend Rowan, the über-irritating genius-boy/Asperger's case.

Calm, Dorri says to herself. *Calm, calm, calm. Keep your eye on the ball.* "Is he always like that?"

Casey turns down the temperature on the cast iron urn of "Homemade Soup" that gets delivered from some warehouse every morning. Kye likes to keep it scorching, but the night before some pot-bellied plumber had threatened to sue Casey for scalding his tongue, lower lip and chin.

"Pretty much," Casey says. "But as far as I can tell, he's never really here at night."

A chubby-armed woman wearing too much makeup for a hardware store stops by the display of cookies. She hugs a round yellow planter, and the sunglasses perched on her head strangely resemble a second set of ears. She clicks her tongue and keeps going.

"Winnie the Pooh," Dorri says. "Don't you think? A grotesquely made-up Winnie."

Casey is still fiddling with the urn, not exactly sure if he's turned the temperature up or down. "What?"

Dorri takes a deep breath, but it doesn't help. "Nothing," she says. "Forget it."

For the rest of the night, they make no further attempt at real conversation. Casey helps her void a soda that tasted flat to a picky guy with a comb-over. He shows her how to heat a meatball supreme. They're all business, which is just fine with both of them.

When Kye had told Casey someone new was starting, Casey couldn't help hoping it might be someone interesting, because he never learned. He knew damn well that things usually turned to shit. He knew any girl he was even half-ass interested in wouldn't be caught dead with their tongue in his mouth. He'd accepted that his sex life was a date with a dirty sock and computer screen. But somehow he never stopped hoping, because one summer some measly thing did happen. Two years ago, they'd rented a cabin at Grand Beach, his parents and him and Rowan, when they were almost fifteen, and he'd got it on with a seventeen-year-old near Lanky's french fry shack. He'd known she was seventeen because her grad date had gone off with her cousin and she was crying her heart out over bottles of hard lemonade. They hadn't actually had sex, but they'd come close, and she'd run her fingers through his hair, told him she loved carrot tops, made him show her his chest to see if it was just as orange. "You're so young," she'd cooed, and he thought he might explode into flames.

Hell, he would've settled for a half-decent guy on his shifts, someone other than Rowan to hang out with. Nearly all his life he'd known Rowan, and all that time Rowan had been a pain in the ass, and yet there he was, always there, and Casey did nothing to get rid of him. Was it too much to ask for a co-worker with maybe some connections, who knew somebody other than the same old, same old?

Apparently it was. Because he got Scarf-face. Who, as it turned out, actually had a name almost as lame as Casey, but who still had the same unibrow, the same skinny ass, the same bitchy expression. Rowan had told him they actually ban those headscarves in France because it's a violation of human rights, a slap in the face for the achievement of separation between church and state. Canadians didn't have to pray in schools anymore. We didn't have to wear a stupid uniform. Why did she always look so frigging smug?

As the night wears on and the measly trickle of customers slows to a drip, getting the cold, modestly covered shoulder begins to get to him. He is a live-and-let-live guy. He couldn't give two shits what she wore on her head. Half the time, people got their panties in a knot about absolutely nothing. You might as well just go ahead and avatar yourself permanently, Rowan liked to say, since everything out there is just a game anyway.

But ignoring someone right beside you, minute after mind-numbingly boring minute, staring out into the garbage-strewn parking lot like it was the frigging ocean at sunset, wasn't just too weird-ass for words. It was rude.

Twice, Casey's father has won City Transit Driver of the Year, and if there is one thing the big, friendly doofus has taught his son, it's that a little bit of chatter never hurt anyone. And besides, he wasn't the one who'd brought up Winnie the frigging Pooh.

He begins putting cheese slices away for the night, slamming the mini fridge drawers as hard as he can. "So do your parents make you wear that thing?"

Casey has no way of knowing that he isn't far off about the concrete ocean vista. Dorri's neighbour, Rain, has been trying to teach her meditation techniques so she can chill the hell out. But that's easy for Rain to say because she'd learned to chant a mantra before she could talk. And it's easy for Rain's parents because they'd inherited some money and could spend a lot of time on spiritual whims.

Dorri shakes her head and pops a black olive in her mouth. "Uh-uh."

This is not what Casey expects. Not the answer, and not the olive. "Then why do you wear it?"

Dorri helps herself to a medium cup and pushes one of the magic buttons. Iced tea descends as if from the heavens until it spills over the sides, pooling at a grated base that lacks proper drainage.

"You pushed large," Casey says.

Dorri pats the little puddle on the floor with her shoe. "No shit."

"So why do you wear it?" Casey asks.

Dorri shrugs a big exaggerated stage-shrug. "Because they hate it."

Casey gets the mop and slops up around her brown suede

clogs. They look like something dirty hippies might wear. "So you don't have to?"

She has to stop herself from asking *don't have to what?* Rain has warned her that there is a fine line between good angry and too angry. "Do you know any Iranian history?"

Casey keeps mopping, spreading iced tea all over the puke-yellow tiles. This is not same old, same old. Scarf-face didn't wear that thing because of some strict Muslim daddy. She didn't talk like an uptight chastity case. She stole from her employer before she'd even finished her first shift.

"No," he says. "I mean, I know they're crazy over there. Like they burn flags and try to get nukes."

She starts laughing then, not exactly at him, but like she's at a loss, like that's all there's left to do.

And the whole way home on his bike, in the frigging tepid rain, he keeps hearing it, that laugh, keeps seeing her laughing face, the way her unibrow stitches together like a worm crawling on a wet sidewalk. The way her lips seemed so hugely pink and her teeth so headlight-white against her dark skin. He can't get over that she of all people is called Dorri, a good name for an animated fish or the adorable dwarf in a storybook. He has no idea yet that in Farsi, Dorri means sparkling like the sun, a fact Dorri views as more of a sick joke than a blessing.

There was so much those two, Casey and Dorri, didn't know. Enough to fill shift after shift under a fluorescent sky, an eternity of dead Friday nights behind the counter/cage.

They don't talk about the fact that he lives north of Portage Avenue, where the aging housing stock is filled primarily with what the government likes to call "working families," along with a good helping of crazy cat ladies, Hells Angels chapters and socially assisted renters who come and go thrown in. Or that she lives on the south side, the mud-bottomed river side, where "professional families" fix up their aging housing stock with custom-made stained glass and kitchen renos that maximize a property's market value. They don't talk about the fact that Casey's mother is the sunny school secretary with a bad haircut and big mouth, or that his father once played on the national water polo team and now drives a bus. Dorri never mentions that her parents are both professional flautists, the only Muslim members of the symphony, who, truth be told, probably worship music more than Allah.

But they do talk. Casey asks questions to fill the empty, high-ceilinged space, to hear a voice that isn't Rowan's. Dorri answers because she can't help it. There is so much to explain.

"Why are you working here if you hate it so much?" Casey asks.

Dorri salts the cucumbers and helps herself. "I need money. A lot of money."

Casey tries not to bite. There are times he thinks she says things just to reel him in, to play up her mystery. She tells him she wears the headscarf because she hates superficiality, hates the way our consumer society treats women like objects. Then the next minute she tells him plastic surgeons in Iran perform more nose jobs than in any other country in the world. She says she hates the extremists and their perverted view of Islam, then she says she quit piano lessons because music is not really a traditional part of Muslim culture.

But like his dieting mother with a piece of cake that isn't even close to her favourite kind, Casey bites anyway. *You have no mind of your own,* Rowan has told him. *You're a cipher.*

"Why do you need money?" Casey asks.

Dorri squeezes honey mustard on a perfect row of cucumber slices. "Because I need to escape that shit-hole school. My friend Rain goes to the Collegiate downtown, where it's reportedly civilized, but pricey. Her parents are potheads but they have money that mine don't. Plus mine won't pay a cent because they think I'm going through some phase and don't want to reward it."

Dorri places a slice on her tongue, like Casey's mother at communion. He's never given much thought to "good" or "bad" schools. Weren't they all the same? You had jocks, brains, outcasts, nobodies; you had teachers who thought they could inspire you and change your life and those who counted the sleeps until summer vacation—call it what you wanted, it was all the same shit. Pick a school, any school, and Rowan would still be a genius and he would still be a nobody.

Casey waits until the row of cucumber slices is gone. "Why don't you just do what they want to get what you want?"

Dorri crunches cucumber, stares at him as if she's lost all hope. Her long nose, wiggling as she chews, looks sharp enough to stab someone. "Listen. This is all I know. If I want to survive next year, I need tuition."

She doesn't mention, or perhaps is barely aware herself, that her one and only reason for being at their school has just graduated. The gorgeous, the gracious, the superior Jagat Kapur was leaving her for McGill. Nationally ranked sprinter, undisputed science fair champion, valedictorian—a brown face beloved by all. He was in a league by himself, larger than life rather than popular, leaving her happy to follow alone and admiring and invisible, eating his dust.

"Do you really think it will be any different?" Casey asks.

Dorri gets a chocolate milk from the cooler. "A university campus is about open minds. It respects different opinions. Believe me, Rain is not your average volleyball cutie. She flashes her unshaved pits every chance she gets."

Now and then, Dorri says something that Casey can't just let go. How can you dress like some oppressed female whose husband thinks you're his property and still talk about unshaved pits?

"But why do you really care?" he asks. "It's not like you're really religious or anything."

Dorri grabs a straw and waves it in front of his nose. "That's not true. You think I haven't read my Quran? You think just because I'm not submissive I don't live by the true principles of my faith?"

She drops the straw and when she bends to get it, her pale blue polo shirt, baggy as a sack, gapes open. Casey can see the upper part of her small breasts, perfectly rounded lobes pushing up from a white sports bra. Her skin is smooth and coffee-coloured.

She jabs him in the chest with the dirty straw. "My faith is about modesty and simplicity and I'm not perfect, but it's what I believe. Some people may call themselves Muslims, but they're not. Too many in the Middle East are ignorant and too many here are sellouts. But at least I'm trying to live what I believe."

Casey knows he should feel guilty for copping a look, but he doesn't. He watches her full pink lips move over the tiny space between her front teeth and wonders how he could have ever thought she was quiet or reserved.

After a few weeks, Dorri starts to put on a little weight from snacks of stolen honey oat bread, and when Rowan tries to get him to call in sick to play Civilization, Casey brushes him off.

"Fine," Rowan says, "go be a cog in the machine. I got worlds to build."

Dorri and Casey speak of each other to no one, which gives an odd weightlessness, an unreality, to their conversations. She floats through his dreams headless and topless, a coffee-coloured mannequin.

"Do you always steal stuff?" he asks her.

She keeps eating olives. "This isn't stealing."

All his life, Casey was taught to play by the rules. His father was a former jock who revoked his son's beginner's licence for a week when Casey failed to signal his turn into the driveway. Where Rowan interrupted the class with random genius facts, Casey had perfect attendance.

"Yes, it is," Casey says.

Dorri stops chewing and sighs. She wonders how one could've lived sixteen years on this planet and given so little thought to things. "This chain makes more money for its owners than either of us can probably hope to make in our lifetimes."

Casey is pretty sure the place is franchised and whoever owns this one ain't getting rich. But he isn't absolutely sure. "It's still stealing," he says.

"You spend too much time playing first-person shooters," she says. "Life is not good guys against bad guys. It's more complex."

Casey swears that her nose gets more beak-like when she talks like that. "You don't know what I play."

Dorri is never quite sure when she's going to hurt his feelings. There's something about him that makes her want to kick him, maybe the puppy thing. Yet she finds herself babbling to him like she hasn't to anyone since she was small and used to follow around her grandfather like he was Allah. Sometimes, it's as if she's carrying the weight of 3,000 years of Persian civilization on her shoulders.

"Listen," she says, "here's what I know. The 1980 revolution in Iran was as much about social equality as it was about religion. My grandparents mostly left because they were worried they'd have to give some of their stuff to dirt-poor farmers."

"Were they loaded?" Casey asks.

Dorri shrugs her shrug. "Like a lot of Iranian expats, they're obsessed with appearances. My mother went to school to become a dermatologist and her parents never forgave her for becoming a lowly musician. My father's mother gets her nails done twice a week and complains about our neighbourhood."

"What does all that have to do with stealing food from your employer?" Casey asks.

"Everything," Dorri says.

They never talked about any future plans, like the fact that Dorri already had completed the first twelve pages of a graphic novel, or that Casey really had no post-secondary plans even though Rowan talked incessantly about the two of them partnering to develop a video game set during the Big Bang. Dorri and Casey never mentioned their days outside of work, how Casey usually slept until the lunch hour, at which time his mother made cheesy scrambled eggs and pork sausages, or that Dorri could regularly sense her mother just outside her bedroom door, picking at her close-cut musician's fingernails, stewing about her hopelessly unattractive, hopelessly stubborn oldest daughter.

But once the silence was breached, not saying anything at all is not really an option. For some reason, both feel the need to fill any lull, any quiet void between them, like those times when you lie in bed and the reality of your own death hits you square between the eyes and the only thing to do is to get rid of that thought, to think hard about something else, small and stupid, like how your gums throb a little after flossing. So Dorri tells him about the time she went with Rain to her family's renovated caboose in a farmer's field and how she almost ran the 200 kilometres home when Rain's parents woke up and began preparing breakfast without any clothes on.

"They don't mind your scarf, so why should you mind their lack of pants?" Casey asks, because he really wants to know.

"Shut up," Dorri says. "Don't tell me you could stand it."

And Casey knows that she's right, but his point is, who is Dorri to judge when they don't judge her? But he doesn't say this, because he knows it will make her testy, like when she talks about her baby sister. She's told him Nina is a French horn prodigy, which is why Dorri dropped the cello, and then the oboe, and took up art.

"Music is a strictly expressive skill," she informs him. "It appeals to our reptilian brains. But visual art or storytelling encompasses the whole of experience, including the intellect. It doesn't matter what the artist looks like, whether they wear clown shoes or a turban, it's about the piece of work and what it has to say."

Casey senses that she pulls most of this out of her ass, but this doesn't bother him much.

Twice, Rowan comes by the sub counter uninvited and orders a cup of water, which he thinks is very funny. He acts as if he's never seen Dorri before, and Casey knows there's a good chance he doesn't actually notice her. When Rowan is intent on something, he can be incredibly dense.

The first time, when he's barely out of earshot, Dorri whacks Casey's shoulder with the back of her hand. "What's his deal?"

"He's obsessed with nutrition," Casey says. "He could tell you everything wrong with that pickle you just ate. He calls these *sulphate sandwiches*."

"How can you stand it?" Dorri asks.

He tells her he's just used to it, tells her Rowan came by because he needs to get away from his older brother, who's home from college and still hates Rowan so much that he pounds on him when no one's looking.

Later that night, Rowan texts Casey from the convenience store, where he's apparently treating himself to sesame snaps: *btw tell s-face that allah is a misogynist pig and see if she fatwa's me.*

Casey texts back: *like u need someone else who wants you dead.*

He touches the whacked spot, which is still slightly pink due to his ridiculously sensitive skin. He wonders how either of those two think they're qualified to call a freak a freak.

As the summer drags on, Dorri and Casey also come to share a few in-jokes, a necessity of the dreary sandwich trade. One night, they notice they have a regular—a giant girl of maybe fourteen who orders the same thing every time: meatball supreme, baked sour cream potato chips, chocolate toffee cookie, large iced tea.

They decide the tiny cubic zirconia letter M around her giant neck stands for meatball, and lay bets on when she will appear, staring up at the menu as if for the first time and then ordering the same-old same-old.

Though there is never a lineup, they compete to see who can make the fastest sandwich. Dorri, not blessed with the manual dexterity of either of her parents, finds her weakness is separating the thin slices of cold cuts without ripping them, while Casey squeezes the condiment bottles so hard they tend to spurt.

He begins to try and guess what's under the headscarf to distract her during competition. "So what, are you bald under there? You got drunk and tattooed your whole head with unicorns, didn't you?"

"Shut up," she says. "Shut up, shut up, shut up."

"Just give me a peek," he says. "I can keep a secret. My mom's hair went all patchy and thin after I was born and she bought this stuff to dye her scalp. You don't have to be embarrassed."

"Shut up."

"Recurring lice?"

"Shut up."

"Bad afro?"

"Shut up. I mean it. I'll charge you with harassment."

Weeks go by and if you were to ask either one of them if they like each other, they would hate you for it, as if you were demanding to know which one farted.

In mid-August, a bright day that somehow smells for the first time like the dry decay of fall, Dorri is quiet, barely makes eye contact, as if they're back at square one. When she can stand it no longer, she follows him to the soup urn and swings him around by the arm. "You want a look? Take a good look, then."

He is very aware of her bony fingers around his bicep. "What the hell?"

She looks momentarily uncertain, an expression he does not recognize at all. "Don't tell me you didn't notice. Don't tell me you're not wondering."

He stares straight into her face for perhaps the first time. There is something different but he doesn't know what. Same sullen lips, same hawk nose, same black eyes. No unibrow.

"Oh," he says.

"It wasn't my decision," she says. "My grandmother blackmailed me."

He keeps staring, as if she's daring him not to look away. The brows now arch like castle doorways over her dark eyelashes. "What do you mean she blackmailed you?"

Dorri hates herself for how she's handling this, hates her need to explain to this freckled idiot, hates her family, hates everyone. "She said she'd contribute to my Collegiate fund if I went and got a wax."

Casey steps away, takes a breath. "Oh. Well, that's good, no? Now you'll have the money."

"Look," she says. "I'm okay with what I look like. It's all a freak of genes. My mother and little sister got the proportions. I look like my paternal grandmother, whose father had money, at least."

He suddenly feels trapped on another planet where he has no idea what's expected of him. Her voice is slightly shaky, as if she's just getting over a cold. "It looks good," he says. "I mean, you look good now."

Dorri hates him most of all. "Just shut up. Okay?"

"I was trying to be nice," he says.

"Well, don't, okay? I was blackmailed."

"Who cares?" he says. "You got what you wanted. She got

what she wanted. I once pretended to go to a whole winter of indoor soccer practice just to make my dad happy. Turns out he didn't even care that much, but what did I know, I was eight. Families suck."

It strikes her that this is the most he's ever told her about himself, and for some reason, this makes her laugh.

"What?" he asks.

"Nothing," she says, still laughing, verging on tears. "Nothing. Families suck."

That night, Dorri writes only one sentence in her journal. *Would I still love Jag Kapur if he weren't so beautiful?*

Casey dreams of plucked eyebrows dancing over coffee-coloured orbs.

Not long after, he comes home after work to find his mother kneeling at the downstairs toilet, staring in the bowl as if it holds the secret to life.

"Are you sick?" he asks. "Where's Dad?"

"You'll find out soon enough," she says. "It'll probably be in the papers."

"What are you talking about?" he asks. "What's the matter with you?"

What she tells him is too impossible to take in. It's as if Casey is trapped in another universe where up is down and yellow is red.

He sleeps through the next day to avoid her, is filled with guilt and relief when no eggs or sausage are forthcoming. He digs out the three badly rolled joints his dad gave him last year so he could "explore in a safe way." Turns out pot mostly makes Casey sleepy, but it's all he has, so he lights up, starts to cough like the half-ass smoker that he is. He emerges to find the house deserted, slinks out to work as if he's the one who's responsible for the snot pouring from his mom's nostrils. When she still worked at the elementary school, she saw a lot of sick or bawling kids come through the office and she had a name for that snotty face: *They'd come at you*, she'd say, dragging two fingers down from her nose to upper lip, *sporting a perfect number eleven.*

He cycles to work through the network of smelly back lanes and it's as if his pedalling feet belong to someone else. The few half-ass tokes of his dad's half-assed weed cannot explain how he feels—he is outside himself, hovering somewhere beneath the low branches that hang down over the lane like Rowan's hair hangs in his eyes. Casey is watching himself as others must see him—a skinny, sweaty ginger on a mid-price bike that's too big for him, the kind of person who will take orders from other people for the rest of his life, the same as his poor puking, balding mother.

By the time he reaches the big-box parking lot he's as faint as a Southern belle in the movies and nearly gets hit by a pickup loaded with drywall and assholes who don't shoulder check. Inside, he slouches down behind the drink cooler, tries to get his head between his knees, only he's not flexible enough.

"What's with you?" Dorri asks.

When he doesn't respond, she crouches down beside him, lightly touches the back of his pimply neck, the skin as white as her grandmother's cold cream. "Hey. You okay? Are you sick?"

And it all comes tumbling out, as awful and uncontrollable as blowing chunks. How his affable buddy-of-a-dad had become infatuated with a regular passenger—a youngish blonde university student, a single mom who probably thought she was being nice, who appreciated all the times he waited for her when she was literally running late. How she had to take out a restraining order against him. How the fat fool still thought he loved her, how he was moving out of their house and leaving his son to pick up the pieces of his stupid, trusting wife of twenty-one years.

He tells her this even though she is possibly the one person who won't find out by other means. In a few weeks, she'll be at her precious civilized campus with some hippie jock named Rain while he is stuck with nowhere to hide. His mother may have been a drama queen about the newspapers, but you can bet she'll be telling anyone who'll listen that her husband is a stalker.

For once, Dorri feels speechless. What do you say to something like this? That his father is a product of an oversexed society obsessed with youth? She runs her thumb along the protruding vertebrae in his neck. "It'll be okay," she says.

Casey looks up, searches her face for something he recognizes. Her breath smells like olives as black as her eyes. They are close enough to feel each other's breath, far closer than ever before, so close he can make out a few dark stubby hairs beginning to grow between her eyes. He takes her head in both hands, tugs hard at the stubborn scarf, pulls her close enough to let his tongue push open those righteously natural pink lips. Then he is up against the cooler, gasping for air, her fist still crushing his abdomen even after she's disappeared.

Seemingly oblivious to it all, M-is-for-Meatball stands in her usual spot by the cookie case, perusing the menu. Dorri takes a deep, meditative breath.

"Have you decided?" she gasps.

For the rest of the week, she assumes she will call in sick for her final shift. After all, the money is in the bank, she has already gotten what she wanted. Her smug, happily married parents have grown weary of dwelling on their Dorri Dilemma and seem content to let the phase play itself out. There is a slight chance, who knows, that Jag Kapur has decided to take the local route for his undergraduate degree, that he will appear before her one day, trailed by a cluster of fawning sophomores sophisticated enough to truly appreciate him. Or perhaps there will be more Jag Kapurs, entire couches-full in the common rooms.

But she does not dream of this. Instead she dreams of her and Casey as children. There she is, ridiculously grown-up nose and lips in an eight-year-old face, running through the back lane behind Rain's house, where they used to play hide-and-go-seek with other neighbourhood kids. Casey has found her and is chasing her as fast as he can with his little paper-white legs, his close-cropped helmet of orange barely moving in the breeze. She's faster but he doesn't let up, just keeps coming until she throws herself onto a patch of green, green grass that appears from nowhere in the middle of the pebbly, skin-shredding concrete. He flops down on top of her, face flaming as his hair, panting like a puppy. "You're it," he says. "You're it."

So she finds herself once again walking through the hideous big-box parking lot, what Rain calls the planet-killing suburban plague. As she passes an ancient, gas-guzzling pickup, a mangy black dog watches her from his perch in the truck bed. He looks so expectant that she stops for a moment and stares back, and then he is bounding towards her, up and over the side of the truck, and she is scrambling back to avoid his flying, filthy bulk. He lands on the unforgiving concrete like a drunk jungle cat, and she backs away slowly, careful not to make more eye contact, rifling through her mental notes of the animal behaviour unit of last year's biology class. But there is no tail wagging, no ear bending, no back arching that gives her a clue. He makes no attempt to follow her, simply watches her go with the same curious, expectant look.

Once again, she finds herself back under those hideous fluorescents, behind that counter/cage one last time, because whatever that dog might think, she is not one to walk away. Her ugly grandmother was also known for not suffering fools gladly.

It's Friday night, but the end of cottage season is nigh. Though it's still sticky hot outside, preparations have begun to close things up, or shut things down, for another long, dead winter. Casey and Dorri must make sandwiches alongside each other as silently as they did that very first shift. She must wait until the bitter end, until the *closing in ten minutes blah blah blah* announcement has been made.

"I thought we were friends."

Heard out loud, just like that, it suddenly seems true enough. But it's too late, because Casey is done with that shit. Last year, he'd known from the beginning that Rowan was the one who'd posted the image, the one that featured Casey the Puppet and "Casey Jr.," side by side. Only Rowan had access to that photo of Casey in the morning, his bright hair plastered to his forehead, his stick arms hanging limply at his sides. Only Rowan would think it was okay to use his obsessive Photoshop skills to burn a friend.

"Hey, you have to laugh at yourself, cut them off at the knees," Rowan had said. "You have to express how you royally don't give a shit."

And only a nobody pussy like Casey would let it go, would decide it was too much trouble to kick Rowan to the curb.

"It just happened," Casey says to her. "Don't flatter yourself."

Dorri can't help it. Such unexpected, uncharacteristic scorn makes her laugh. "Wow. Stress makes you feisty."

Casey stares. He is either going to hit her or start to cry. "My mom's hair is falling out again. She says it's stress."

Dorri can't stop laughing. She imagines his mother giving new meaning to the phrase *pulling your hair out*.

"I'm sorry," she says. "I'm sorry."

She takes him by the bony elbow, leads him behind the drink cooler. She unties the knot behind her neck, lifts the creamy silk scarf from her head, holds it up like a flag of surrender.

Her hair is not long, like he imagined. It's all one length and it hugs her sharp jawline. Suddenly free, a few strands fall over her right eye. He brushes it aside and she lets him.

"There," she says. "Okay? No big deal. It's hair."

Once, a long, long time ago, before he met Rowan, Casey

found a small stone at the beach near his grandparents' hobby farm. On a sunny day it seemed so black it was almost blue, and for the whole summer he carried it in his pocket so he could rub that impossibly smooth, shiny darkness whenever he felt like it. Then it was run through the washer, and his mom thoughtlessly tossed it, and he forgot about it.

"Okay," he says.

Dorri expertly reties the scarf and goes to count twenties. "Okay then. We're good."

Casey doesn't move, wonders if maybe he was right to hope all along, maybe life is full of surprises.

Little Emperor

Four Facts and Some Speculation

1. The world's two most populated countries—China and India—together constitute nearly 40% of the world's population.
2. Toilet paper was invented in China in the late 1300s. It was for emperors only.
3. The Three Gorges Hydroelectric Dam spans the Yangtze River and is the largest dam in the world. It is also the most controversial, its construction having been marred by corruption charges, human rights violations, technological difficulties, and the dramatic environmental changes it has caused.
4. China's "one child" policy has contributed to female infanticide and has created a significant gender imbalance. There are currently 32 million more boys than girls in China. In the future, tens of millions of men will be unable to find wives, prompting some scholars to suggest that this imbalance could lead to a threat to world security.

Historians speculate that as the Chinese population grew, people had to conserve cooking fuel by chopping food into small pieces so that it could cook faster. These bite-sized foods eliminated the need for knives and, hence, chopsticks were invented.

I have been inside many days, so many I've lost count, when the screaming begins. I am in the kitchen, staring at the mountain of soiled dishes, so many I've lost count of them as well. It is a faint scream, if there can be such a thing—a scream from far away. But it is coming from below, so is really quite close, one floor or ceiling away, depending how you look at it.

I have heard nothing, not one thing, from inside this apartment until the screaming. This is what they call them here—the individual spaces are "apartments" and the entire buildings are "apartment blocks." This block, constructed many decades ago, probably when China still had an emperor and who knows who ran things here, is built of brick and is oddly silent—soundproof, they call it. One night, not long after I arrived, before the attack, the people next to me, my neighbours, they had many, many people over, played music at high volumes, and I heard nothing until I stepped out to go buy some tea. This is how I think of my time here now—before the attack (BA) and after the attack (AA), like Christians measure time based on the birth and death of their crucified saviour.

It's hard to believe someone can scream so long without taking a breath. It is really quite astonishing. She must have fine lungs, must have spent her life in the crisp, healthy air of Canada. In China, they throw buildings up out of cardboard and the air is sick. My parents, they laughed and laughed at the name of this place—WI-NEE-PEG—but not too hard, because it is my ticket to success. They would stand in awe at the luxurious space I have in this one apartment, this completely soundproof space, except for the faint screaming. They would not believe the metres and metres of real estate devoted to parked cars. They would not believe a city could have so many trees, so many you think you see a forest from the tenth floor. But they don't ask about such things. Instead they go on about problems at work, gossip about my old schoolmates. They make demands: "Speak to us. Show us your English."

If they only knew! They go on and on and I tell them nothing. For how can I explain to them what I cannot explain to myself? Like how many days has it been since I have left this apartment? How long have I been taking the candy-coloured pills to *manage the pain*? The doctor, not the first one, who did the surgery, but the second, who did what he called "follow-up," uttered that precious phrase—manage the pain. But it was Kyla who helped me to understand. It was Kyla who appeared at the bedside like a guardian spirit, a Christian angel with a gift for languages whose sole purpose was to ease the pain.

Her lips were a little thin and her shoulders a little broad, but she was there and she was mine, and she seemed the perfect woman. "My Chinese is spotty," she'd said. "But I'm just a volunteer and I'm better than nothing."

My mother, had she known, would have clucked her tongue at Kyla's peasant stock, an unwanted second girl abandoned amongst the sweet potatoes at some market in Guangzhou province. But neither of them, not my ancestor-obsessed mother nor my businessman father, would scarcely believe the privilege that those plucked from the orphanages by Western parents now know: the pretty Chinese-speaking nannies and trips overseas, the houses with backyard pools and children's playrooms, the designer clothes and private piano lessons. They would not believe it, have not asked. And I could not explain to them how Kyla's spotty, accented Chinese was like birdsong to me in my time of need.

Now, I listen with great concentration. The screaming has

stopped. There is a knock. For a brief moment, I think it is my father, rapping his knuckle against my skull. *Xaio, get a hold of yourself. We are practical people. We are talking about your future.*

But there is another voice, through the door. "Chow? You there, man?"

It's Albert, who calls me Chow, and I have not corrected him. "Yes," I shout from the kitchen. "I'm here."

He opens the door with his caretaker's key and walks in without removing his shoes. "Chow?"

"I'm here," I say, and he follows my voice, puts a plastic bag full of food and my change from the twenty dollars on the counter. Without looking, I know the bag is full of frozen dinners, instant noodles, and instant soup, things I imagine he eats himself. Each of them could be eaten directly from the container, but I do not do this, because my mother's voice also haunts me. *Food is meant to be eaten from porcelain, not paper. You don't live on the street.* But either way, it makes no difference, because I have no appetite. I heat, I dump into a dish, I pick, I dump into the garbage, I add to the foul mountain.

"You look like shit," Albert says.

Other than the murmuring, owl-faced nurse who came twice to change my dressing, he is the only person I have seen since leaving the hospital AA. He was here when the cab arrived with my bag full of *pain managers*. He walked me up the stairs, handed me a new key. "I changed the lock. They'll probably watch the pawn shops for your electronics."

I had stared dumbly, and he had gestured so I might understand—hand to his ear like a phone, fingers typing on an invisible laptop.

Still, I could not manage a response to the large man beside me, skin dark as a Mongolian mountain herder's, black hair long and loose as the ones who pounded me into the pavement, over and over, until everything was black and dark.

Little Emperor

Gangbangers, Kyla had named them. Most likely a rite of initiation, an act of violence to move up the ranks of their organization. They were Aboriginal people, she'd said, Native Canadians. She knew about this because her father had written some kind of history book on their plight. Their land had been taken and they lived poorly. That's why so many of them were in hospital and in trouble.

On that awful morning, as I stood there without friend or family by my side, Albert must have thought I had become halfwitted, forgotten every word of English I had ever known. He took the newly cut key back from my limp hand and let me in. "The little fuckers really roughed you up, eh."

Now, he puts his hand on my shoulder and I feel I might collapse under the weight of that milk-fattened arm. I try not to notice the mysterious blue-green Roman letters—*K.A.T.*—across his wrist, not unlike the lightning bolt I'd seen on the fat one's calf, the one who'd pulled me up only to smash me down again.

This is another thing my mother and father would never believe—the many, many numbers of tattoos in this place. They are everywhere: on nameless gangbangers, on caretakers named Albert, on perfect women named Kyla. I swear I can hear my mother's snort. *The Chinese symbol for peace? I don't care what it is. It's tawdry.*

Albert squeezes a little and I try not to wince. "It's been more than two weeks," he says. "You got those crutches there, you got to get out of this place. Go take a walk, go buy yourself some stir-fry or something. They have a wok place in the mall there."

I fear I might begin to tremble uncontrollably, and so I will him to leave. *Go. Go now. Your business is done here. Can't you see that once I begin trembling I may never stop?*

"It's not bad," he says. "You get a free egg roll when you buy a drink."

Then I remember. "I must ask you. Do you hear? The yelling?"

He releases my shoulder, stands quietly. He listens. "Yelling?"

"There is yelling," I say, but even as the words come out I know they are wrong. There was screaming.

He listens for another moment, smiles. "I don't hear anything."

"No," I say. "Before. Yelling."

"Probably kids outside," he says.

I shake my head, *no, no, no,* but really, I nod, smile a little, because it is no use, I am alone here with no family or friends in WI-NEE-PEG and it is no laughing matter. I let him go, lock the door behind him, check the deadbolt, let him leave me with my terror, and my mountain of dried-on stink, and my phantom screams.

The ache in my ribs makes it hard to breathe, but it is the pain in the knee that makes sleep so unpleasant I count the minutes until I will be able to take the next little orange pill, and then let it drag me away into nightmares. The things that sneak up from behind and then pounce have expanded to the absurd. Little yellow-haired girls in braids who turn out to have wolf teeth; fast-food teriyaki cooks with cleavers; tremendous, roaring tsunamis that somehow reach my land-locked hell. My sleep is drugged, false, fitful, and when I wake, the distant screaming has returned.

The clock's gleaming red numbers read 2:20. It is past midday and I have nothing to show for it. Nothing but a dream of being stalked by an old lady with claws for fingers.

Be a man. It's again my father's voice. And this makes me want to scream myself, to laugh like one gone mad, because he is one to talk. Who is he to judge that I want to shit my pants like an infant? I am not cut out for this. Just ask my mother, the historian. During the Imperial days, my ancestors hid behind royalty, held their silk hems, wiped their royal asses. Then later, when the revolution came for them, they ran to the collective farms, asked how high they should jump, how many friends they should denounce. Yes, I come from a long line of soft, sickly cowards.

The screaming starts and stops, starts and stops, then carries on for what seems like one whole minute. I reach for the phone Kyla brought to me when she was still my angel—*an extra lying around,* she'd said, *pay as you go.* I call Albert on this precious get-well gift but it rings and rings until I throw it across the room.

I slide out from beneath the sweat-stained sheets, drag myself awkwardly from the bed, pad stiff and flat-footed across the wooden floor, almost faint as I bend myself in two, pick up the still ringing phone. My ancestors were also not cut out for such outbursts. *We are calm and practical people.*

The screaming continues until 3:06 sharp. I spend the rest of the day waiting. I call Albert twice more and the phone rings and rings, but I do not lose my temper. I do nothing, don't dare venture out the south door, where you can almost see the university from the sidewalk. Nor out the east door into the shadow of office buildings, where the businessmen ignore you on the way to the gym, where the shopping mall right in the middle of the city has more empty real estate to lease than all of Beijing. My father would not believe the empty space to be had. He would not believe that not far outside the north door, one street corner from the businessmen and their high-priced sneakers, one could be robbed of one's belongings, health, peace of mind. Kyla said there is no Chinese word for *geh-toe* and that you don't just find them in American rap music. Because that is what one thinks when one thinks of gangsters, big black men in big American cities, with big black guns in big American cars. Kyla called the people of the *geh-toe,* here and everywhere, the *dis-en-fran-chised,* but I did not exactly get her meaning.

The bruised ribs make it painful to sit for any period, so I stand at the kitchen counter and go to Kyla's Facebook page.

Perhaps two weeks ago, after I'd given him detailed instructions, Albert had come to the door with my credit card and the new laptop.

"I bought myself one, too," he'd said. "Hope you don't mind."

I had not noticed his smile, so relieved I was to regain my connection to the world. "With this same card?" I asked.

He'd laughed, ruining some of my relief. "I shouldn't joke. You're in rough shape, man."

But the very next day, Kyla graciously agreed to be my Facebook friend and this has become the one ray of sunshine in my dreary existence. I now know her favourite style of shoe, her favourite song from the 1990s, her favourite brand of body lotion. I have seen pictures of her friends, some Chinese adoptees like herself, and some even more attractive. I find very little new information, except two picture of her at *the lake*, which she explained to me in the hospital. In WI-NEE-PEG, many people have summer homes near the region's many lakes, and when they go on holiday they simply say *I am going to the lake*, as if they sleep floating on water. In one picture, Kyla is raising a glass of what looks like tomato juice at the camera and in the other, she is jumping off a wooden pier, arms and legs spread wide as a star. At least I think this is her, because it is a rear view.

There is also a message from my mother, which I choose to ignore. She would think Kyla's behind looks too large, and would refuse to believe that ordinary office workers might own summer homes. For my parents have no interest in the West other than how it might enhance my future. They are proud Chinese. They would be truly outraged about my situation, about how the university could be located so near the *geh-toe*, an innocent foreign student attacked one block from his front door, and just two weeks before term begins! They would wring their hands and then send for me without delay. And yet I do not let them. I sit here alone, without friends or family, waiting.

I swallow a little orange pill and sleep some more. When I

wake, it is 9:11, and my stomach aches from hunger, but the beef soup tastes of nothing but salt and dead animal. The potatoes are as uniformly square as playing dice and I only manage several spoonfuls. BA, I used to have too much fat. Too much mother love, my Beijing neighbour liked to say. But I had become not a bad cook myself, and three times in this apartment, BA, I took a taxi to the Asian market, the one the others at the university orientation had recommended. I fixed myself three feasts for one, and even promised myself to invite the others next time.

Not long ago, Albert had wrapped his fingers around my bicep and laughed. "You're looking pretty thin there, man. Do I have to open those cans for you, too?"

I wanted to take him down like in the movies, the small man with superior skills who easily defeats his bigger opponent. But I smiled through my anger. "Before, too fat. Now, I am slim."

I go to the window and look north into the night. Many evenings, after the workday is finished and the busy traffic time has died down, I have seen Albert walk first a little west, towards the university, then north until he disappears down the narrow lane that is hemmed in by a brick office building and a low-grade sushi establishment. It is the same lane of my attack. I can almost see the very spot from my window. He always returns via the same route shortly after the dusk turns to dark. I know this because I have seen him, and because he never answers his phone before then. It just rings and rings until it is time to turn on a lamp.

I wait until 10:08.

"Yeah, Chow," he says. "You okay?"

I choose my words carefully. "You come here. Please."

There is a silence. Then: "What do you need?"

The phone is too difficult. Is this so hard to understand? "You come here. Please."

There is a silence. "Give me a minute."

I wait at the door, at the ready, hear his heavy footsteps as they approach. I open the deadbolt before he can knock. He is wearing what he always wears at this time—a sweatshirt with the sleeves cut away, and jeans that have been cut into shorts. His big feet are bare and his legs are as hairless as my own. He stinks like my bed sheets.

I point at the floor. "Down there," I say. "There is screaming."

He listens dutifully as if this is the first he has heard of it.

"Not now," I say.

"When?"

"The day," I say. "The afternoon."

"You sure?"

"Yes, I am sure," I say. "Not loud sound, but screaming."

I step aside so he may come in, but he remains in the doorway. "I don't know, Chow. There's no other complaints."

"I am sure," I say. "I here all day. I hear it." Hear and here—two words that sound the same but are different—it is the first time I have used them correctly.

Albert runs his meaty fingers through his sweaty hair, sighs so deep the exhale sputters through his closed lips. "Okay, Chow. I'm just wondering if you're okay up here all by yourself. Maybe you need some help or something."

"I here all day," I say again. "I hear it."

Albert smiles like I am a child who is insisting on a later bedtime. "Yeah, yeah, okay. I'll look into it. Okay?"

"Where you go, at night?" I ask.

He laughs. "Oh, you seen me? You spying on me?"

I don't understand.

"That's my night job. I play ball with the little punks at Freight House."

"What kind of fight house? What is this?"

He smiles. "No. Freight House. But it's not a house-house. It's an old railway warehouse or something."

"You make money to play basketball?"

"Pocket change," he says.

I don't understand and I am sick to death of this. The humiliation is too much. I hate the West and all its cheesy-smelling inhabitants. But I ask anyway. "What is this?"

He pulls coins from his jeans. "Pocket change. Little bit of money."

"This punks," I say, "they do this to me? You know them?"

"Christ, I hope not," he says. "But I promise you, I find out who did this to you, their ass is mine. They may do their time, but their ass is mine."

I wonder if the Aboriginals have the Christian guilt, or if they worship dead ancestors as we do. Or maybe their gods are animals, like the South Asians. But no matter what, he is being paid to manage the punks in the *geh-toe* and he is failing. Just like in the factories back home. The Party tries to improve the dismal conditions but it's not enough, the workers keep heading to the roof and jumping to their death. So all they can do is put up a net around the building.

The West has failed the visiting international student. So all Albert can do is bring me food I cannot eat. It would all be laughable if it weren't so painful.

I dream that the walls have come to life and are closing in on me, hugging tighter and tighter until dusty plaster thumbs are plugging my nostrils and gagging my throat. Yet I am in two places at once, for I am also watching my parents, still in Beijing, watching me dying online and taking turns screeching in horror at my plight. All their work, all their savings, all their lives, they have poured into this doomed son who will soon be squished like a helpless gnat. No fighting crickets proudly battling to the death for our family. We will rail for mercy until the end.

When I finally wake to pass water, it is past noon and the regular afternoon screaming has already begun. Perhaps it is my parents, I think, all the way from Wangujing Street, horrified that my English has made so little progress AA. How is one to get ahead these days without the language of global commerce? *There is so much work still ahead, so much catch-up for each and every one of us, scholar and peasant alike, for the waking giant that is China.*

I flush and the water in the bowl swirls and swirls, grows higher and higher, swirling ominously until it spills the banks of the seat. I wonder if I am still dreaming, if this time the flood has come and I will begin to gasp and snort beneath the rising deluge as my parents wave their hands in desperate frenzy. *We don't understand! We won't believe it! How could this happen to our only son?* But my toes are wet with actual water, my pajama bottoms growing soggy at the hems, and I am as helpless as my wailing parents. Through the centuries my ancestors have aimed to avoid this, always kowtowing to the right people at the right time—ancient scholars and court gadflies, party apparatchiks, CEOs—anything to avoid fixing their own toilets.

I grab my bath towel and plunge into the toilet bowl as far as my armpit, shove the towel into the drain hole as far as it will go. The hissing continues but the rising stops and I go to call Albert.

But my phone is nowhere to be found. Which is disturbing to me, perhaps more than the loss of appetite or the fear of outside or the nightmares. Because BA, I was a very organized person.

It takes fifteen minutes to find the phone, which had fallen behind the garbage bin in the kitchen. I call Albert, let it ring, call again. I lose count of how often I do this. The screaming stops and I want to take a little orange pill but am afraid to sleep. I check Kyla's Facebook page and there is a picture of her holding up a large scaly fish nearly three-quarters her size. There is a caption that seems to suggest she threw this giant catch back into the lake, which could not be right. I am suddenly so tired of not understanding that I almost open a message from home, but resist at the last moment. I am barely surviving as it is, and my parents' devoted concern in Chinese characters will leave me screaming like the one downstairs.

By the time Albert finally comes with his toolbox it is 4:44. I follow him into the bathroom, then step back into the hall, for he is a big man.

"Holy Christ," he says. "What'd you do here, Chow?"

"I plug the water," I say.

He removes the lid from the top of the toilet and stops the hissing, then reaches in the bowl and pulls out the dripping towel. He throws it into the bathtub and it makes a deep, satisfying *thud*. "You sure you're old enough to be on your own, Chow? Maybe you need a roommate or something."

I talk to his broad, bent back. "I eighteen," I say. "I have student visa."

He studies the inside of the tank, plays with what look like rubber hoses.

"How you know how to do this?" I ask.

Albert keeps fiddling inside the tank as he talks. "I took some courses at the college, but I never finished. Which was fucking stupid, because plumbers make it hand over fist these days. But I was young. I didn't care. All I needed was enough cash to have a good time."

I nod like I understand, because my parents had warned me of Chinese who end up just this way. They have parents who are wealthy enough to lengthen the leash and give them freedom, and many times they grow rebellious and decadent, end up into hard drugs. *Like the days the courtly rich killed themselves with opium,* my mother said, *and their lives are ruined.* Or sometimes they stay in the West and leave their family altogether.

Albert looks into his toolbox. He looks into the tank. He turns to me. "I don't got the part I need. Can you not flush for tonight?"

"You don't fix?" I ask.

He scratches his head, stares at his feet. For the first time, I notice that his front teeth are quite crooked. "Just for tonight. Don't flush, okay? Just leave it. Don't flush."

My bony hands are clenched into fists as he leaves. Because perhaps Albert is not just doing a bad job keeping his people from making trouble. Perhaps he is also not a good caretaker. He is a failure and so I am stuck with more stink when I have plenty of stink already.

I am dreaming of a plunger that has come to life. It has attached itself to me, is trying to suck my face from my skull, when I hear the knocking. For a moment, I believe it's my father, tapping my head with his knuckle. *Hello? Anybody in there? Do you not see how ridiculous you are, son? Your nightmares are laughable! You think you're the only one who's ever suffered? For all our sakes, you must get a hold of yourself!*

But the knocking continues, louder now, stubborn. Like the ringing of the phone after Albert left, shaking the night with its persistence. I did not give in, though, for I knew it was them. They had tracked me down to finish me off. The punks were calling to invite me back to the scene of the crime. *Come, Xaio. Come see. We've got sexy Asian ladies who like a good time and a buffet of Chinese favourites. There is kung pow duck, the very dish your mother made you upon your leaving. Come, come.* They think they can seduce me back to the alley where it happened, between the walls of innocent beige brick, where before the red flashing lights arrived the ghost of a black dog came to lick my wounds as I lay bleeding. But they thought wrong. I hid the phone in a suitcase stuffed with nothing but a winter parka, the expensive down-filled immensity my mother insisted she buy for me.

"Xaio Trang. It is the Winnipeg Police Service. We would like to speak together with you."

The voice is not my dialect, but it is my language. It is calm and very masculine, a voice that dutiful Chinese sons cannot resist. I am out of bed, in my sleep robe, padding barefoot to the door before my brain even knows what my broken body is doing.

Then they are inside, just like that. The chain, the deadbolt, the lock are opened and they are here, one large moon-faced Asian man and one large yellow-haired woman in matching uniforms, sitting tight together on the small sofa.

"We are sorry to rise you from bed, Xaio," the man says. "We tried telephoning."

He has Chinese eyes, but his nose is large, his hair almost wavy, and I wonder if he is part Caucasian. Perhaps his father is a curly-haired Russian who ordered himself a submissive Asian wife from Shanghai. The woman is perhaps Northern Viking stock, with big man-like hands and doll-like features.

"How are you, Xaio?" she asks. Her voice is deep and silky. If we danced, my head would become buried in her big womanly breasts.

I tighten the robe around myself. "I good," I say, and can hear my father laughing. *Already telling the women what they want to hear. See, you can be a man.*

The man smiles and his teeth look too big and white for his face. "School initiates soon, yes? It is excellent to sleep now, to look after your well-being, before study time begins."

I nod, yes. His Mandarin is almost less intelligible than Kyla's. What poor, backward province could his mother have come from?

He leans forward, as if to reach for my hand, but does not. "But we are here to tell you about the investigation is proceeding. We some persons in for questioning right now."

"You have caught the punks?" I ask.

Officer Blondie smiles, looks at me as if I am her son, and I must stop myself from diving into her bosom.

"Well, we are making progressive," Officer Half-Breed says. "We have recovered your telephone, and it seems the persons who did this to you are feuding. We are hearing a multitude of things. But the persons are talking, and this is good."

I nod. I want him to shut up and leave me be with Officer Blondie. I want to rest my head in her bosom and ask her about these gangbangers, the ones Kyla said are neglected by their parents so band together like posses in Hollywood's American West. I want to ask her how those pledged as blood brothers, who commit atrocious acts in league together, could betray each other. What more do they have than loyalty to each other? Was this not the true shame of Mao's revolution, forcing children to turn on parents, or brother on brother? What is left once we've begun to betray those closest to us?

"You sure you're okay?" Officer Blondie asks. "Do you understand?"

I nod. I want both of them gone now, for there is no way Officer Blondie has the answers I seek. Allowing myself to be consumed by her ample white flesh would solve nothing.

"Yes, I fine," I say. "I understand. Thank you. Thank you for your good work."

This seems to satisfy them, because Officer Half-Breed and Officer Blondie both rise up from the small sofa, laughing a little as they jostle together. Perhaps they are like in the movies, partners who are friends and maybe more.

When they are gone, I feel strangely awake, more awake than in many days. I get the laptop and sit on the sofa where it's still warm from the ample white bum. My ribs don't ache as much as they once did, but my heart is strong. The lies pour out as easily as the toilet had overflowed. It's like I'm writing a story, and as I write, I begin to believe.

Hi Mother, hi Father. You must be wondering what happened to your son! But there was no real need to worry. I had electronic difficulties that turned out to be serious (the systems are different here in Canada!), and I have had to replace my phone and computer. This does mean I've had to spend some money, but again, no need to worry. Food and accommodation here are more affordable than we thought and I shouldn't run out. As I told you before, I am just one street from the university, so can walk for free! I miss Mother's kung pow shrimp very much. So much food here is processed ... you wouldn't recognize me I've become so slim!

Still, perhaps it is a good thing I have no gift for languages. My friend An may have mastered English right there in Beijing, but I believe this stay in Canada may be the experience of a lifetime.

I promise your faith in me will not be wasted. X

By the time I'm done, my heart is thumping like a jackhammer on an early Beijing morning, telling all it's time to get up and build the nation. I begin to wonder if it is possible for a heart to explode from adrenalin when it suddenly strikes me that I am starving.

I fish the phone from its parka cocoon and call Albert.

"It Xaio," I say. "I give money, you go to Asian Market for me. Okay?"

He does not respond. It took many tries before he answered, and I think I hear a lady's voice in the background, not deep and smooth like Blondie's, but sweet and teasing.

"Come on, Chow," he says. "You been before, haven't you? You need to get out."

Albert has never turned me down before. I'm not prepared for this. "I see, yes. But I no want to."

"How am I supposed to know what to buy?" he asks.

"I write in Chinese," I say. "You take to them."

"Anyone ever tell you that you make it hard to feel sorry for you, Chow?"

Thump, thump, thump, goes my heart. I don't understand and I don't care. "So you go?" I ask.

There is a sigh. I can see him running his hand through his

hair, hear the sweet voice murmuring. "I don't know, Chow. I got a lot on my plate right now."

But I am a desperate, starving man. I don't give up. "There is still screaming," I say. "In afternoon."

There is another sigh. Sweetie sighs, too, or perhaps it is more of a groan.

"Where is this Asian market?" Albert asks.

Then I know that I am victorious, that his guilt is more powerful than his lust. "It far," I say. "I give you cab fare."

I wait all that night and all the next morning for him to come, but my family can be very patient when we must be. For really, I would say it is the patient, and the pliable, more than the brave, who survive adversity. I pace the worn wooden floors like a soldier on guard. I strip my bed of its smelly sheets and lie robe-less against the cool, naked mattress. I ignore all the messages from home that I have been ignoring for weeks. I read only one, one that is brand new and flies forth from the screen like a dove taking flight.

"How is the knee, Xaio?" KylaSmyla ☺

Four simple English words that somehow change everything, bring a new dawn into my blind-darkened world.

How is it, Kyla? It hurts! Very much, thank you! Thank you, my angel!

When Albert knocks and leaves the grocery bags in the hallway, I am not even insulted.

"Gotta go, man." He waves over his shoulder. "Enjoy."

All afternoon, I chop. Celery and water chestnuts, cauliflower and cashews—none are spared the blade. I work around the precarious mountain of dishes, letting no obstacle get in my way. I think of Kyla, how she spoke to me in a charming combination of broken Mandarin, English, and pantomime, made me laugh until it hurt unbearably with tales of her return to Guangzhou province. *Pretty much everyone stared, and some came right up, took my hand, took my white mother's hand. It was nice, but a little like being the main attraction at a petting zoo. Down the Yangtze, it was as beautiful as I imagined, but my stomach was off so I hurled, snapped a photo, hurled, snapped a photo. Many of the women were so gorgeous, so stylish, but what I loved was that they picked their noses anywhere, anytime! On the bus, on the street, they daintily hold up their newspaper as if no one can see them digging around in there like they're looking for diamonds.*

Such an enticing girl, this Kyla, who is so Chinese, but so not. It's no wonder the grannies on the street couldn't resist coming over to have a little poke just to see if she was real. *I'm volunteering at the hospital because I've been given so much, and I want to give back. And the best schools like that kind of stuff. And it's good to practise my Mandarin, because it's rustier than my French. My one indulgence is those awful vampire novels. I think they literally feed on the sick romantic in all of us.* It's as if one could spend a lifetime exploring her mysteries, and my littered kitchen counter becomes a rainbow of sugar peas and baby carrots, pink shrimp and yellow pepper. How long has it been since I've eaten such riches? Two weeks, two months, two years? *My dad is more of a Mediterranean guy, but I thought the cuisine of Guangzhou was incredible. How can the Chinese be so skinny and so obsessed with food? I think I got sick because I couldn't stop eating.* The sizzle of oil in the pan, the grassy smell of bok choy hitting the heat, makes me so homesick I could cry.

There is knocking at the door and my father interrupts the charming Kyla. *The blubbering must come to an end, son. Don't let us down now.*

It's Albert. "Can I come in?"

I am on the verge of tears but I swallow them down like foul medicine. He sinks down in Officer Blondie's seat and looks around as if it's his first visit. "Smells good."

I don't trust myself to speak, so only smile.

"Just thought you'd like to know," he says. "The lady downstairs, she was off her meds. I went and talked to her and she seemed fine, and the apartment next door's empty until the end of the month. But they left me this phone number for her worker, and he went and took her to the psych ward."

"Meds?" I ask.

"Medicine," he says. "She had medicine to control stuff like the screaming, but then she didn't take it. That's why you heard her."

"They take her to hospital?" I ask.

"Yeah," he says. "Same one as you. This block is a gong show."

Kyla told me that China is the only place on earth where more women kill themselves than men. *The poison of choice is agricultural fertilizer.* Perhaps they all wish they'd been abandoned at the market.

"Please," I say. "You join me for food?"

He clasps his giant hands behind his head, and his beefy, muscled arms are impressive. This is a people who don't need fancy martial arts to stand a chance. He would be a good match for Officer Blondie. "Nah, I just ate," he says.

But I am so filled with relief that I'm not crazy, so full of hope for the first time in how long—two weeks, two months, two years?—that I cannot bear to be alone. "Please, yes. I made much."

I don't give him a chance to resist. I go to the kitchen, scrub out some bowls, fill them heaping with my afternoon's labours. My knee throbs but I pay it no heed, proceed to lay out the feast on the low, build-it-yourself, Chinese-manufactured table that came with the apartment. In Canada, they call it a *coffee table*. I place a plate and fork in front of Albert. "Dig in," I say.

He laughs, and for a few minutes, there is silence. I eat like a man who's been on the verge of eating his dead seatmate after a plane crash. The chopsticks can't reach my lips fast enough.

"It's good," Albert says. "You're a good cook, Chow."

I nod. "Chinese like their food."

We concentrate on eating some more.

"It's funny," Albert says. "I used to watch all those kung fu movies and I kind of wanted to go there. They always had those misty mountains and really tall, bendy trees."

"Bamboo," I say. "Bamboo bends easily in wind."

Albert pushes his plate away, laughs, resumes his strong-man pose. "Christ, I wasn't even hungry, man."

I smile, wonder if I will be sick like Kyla, feasting so well after such a long fast. But I cannot stop, will not stop, because it is a new dawn.

"You know, Chow," Albert says, "you should feel good. You maybe saved that woman. She was in real trouble there."

I nod. But I don't feel good. I feel unafraid, and I look hard at Albert the ball-playing caretaker, because it's as if for the first time, I am observing a truly good man. He is not trying to be stoic or clever or brave or loyal. He is not trying to be anything. He is simply good.

And I think of this picturesque Chinese countryside in the movies. I'm sure Kyla would not believe it, but she has almost certainly seen more of rural China than I. My ancestors have been city people for generations and are not ones to holiday. Only a handful of times have I experienced this countryside of the stories and tourists.

But once, on a school field trip to some temple I can no longer name, the view took my breath away. It was early morning on the bus, all of us students still sleepy, and a mist hung over the rolling rice paddies. As we travelled, it was if the noise and towers of the city were wiped clean with a brushstroke, only to reveal a soft dream of static clouds and slow-flowing waters. And I suddenly want to take Kyla there, to this silly, fleeting dreamland of my boyhood, proudly introduce her to my loving parents despite her broad shoulders and lowly lineage.

"Hey, Chow, you drifting on me?"

I smile. "I have eaten too much."

But really, that isn't it at all. For perhaps it's not true that the

Chinese are not romantics. Perhaps I am simply the first one in my family.

It's Me, Tatia

Five Facts
That Weren't Generally Taught
in Canadian Schools
until the 21st Century

1. For six weeks in the summer of 1919, the city of Winnipeg was crippled by a massive general strike. Frustrated by unemployment, inflation, and poor working conditions, factory workers, police officers, retail clerks, telephone operators, fire fighters—pretty much all those employed by business or government—joined forces to shut down services.

2. On June 21, 1919, which came to be known as Winnipeg's Bloody Saturday, strikers pushed over and set fire to a streetcar. The Royal North-West Mounted Police attacked the crowd of strike supporters gathered outside city hall, killing two and injuring 30. They followed the crowd as it dispersed through the streets, beating protesters with baseball bats and wagon spokes.

3. Strike leaders—mostly British, but also a few Russian Jewish immigrants—were arrested and imprisoned. Workers gained little as a direct result of their walking off the job. But several strike leaders were elected, from jail, to the Manitoba legislature, and R.B. Russell High School and the provincial Wordsworth building are named after them today.

4. The General Strike left a legacy of bitterness and controversy among organized labour groups across Canada. It sparked a wave of increased unionism and militancy, and sympathetic strikes erupted in centres from Amherst, Nova Scotia to Victoria, British Columbia.

5. Around the same time as this labour unrest was occurring, the Canadian government was removing thousands of Aboriginal children from their rural homes and placing them in distant boarding schools, often against their families' will. In order to train the children to become productive members of European Christian society, their native language, dress, and culture were forbidden. Many suffered physical, emotional, and sexual abuse at the hands of their teachers and caregivers.

Never got found, never got found, never got found.

Some glass breaks down on the street, and then you stick your head in the door.

"You all right? Why you up? You have trouble breathing?"

I must've made a noise, cried out, god knows why, because it's the same every night, the beer bottles, or the barking, or

It's Me, Tatia

the sirens, waking me up in the middle of god knows when. It's always the same now, woken up by the slightest little thing, like a cat, always dozing, always waking up.

This time, though, I'm all the way up, in the olive green chair by the window.

"Why you not in bed?"

Go away, it's not your business, I want to say, but I hold my tongue. How did I get into the green chair?

"You gave us a scare before," you say, still in the doorway. "You go out that door, wander away, what if we can't find you? What you thinking? Huh?"

I remember now. I could feel your hands, your little brown hands, no bigger than a child's, shaking as you led me back, gripping hard with those little fingers.

Back in the room, you'd put on the television, filled a foot basin with hot water.

"See? It's your favourite," you'd said. "Cops and robbers. That one there, in the toque, he looks like bad news."

You'd fidgeted with your little necklace the way you always do when you don't know what to do next, but this time it had reminded me of something. *Never got found,* my mind kept repeating, *never got found, never got found.*

I'd seen something out there in the dark. But what was it? Someone was crying maybe, but who?

Now, in the middle of the night, all I know is that you won't leave until I say something, let you know I haven't died on your watch.

"I'm fine. This housecoat is warm. I'm fine here."

You don't go away, just stand in the doorway fidgeting, moving the silly little cross back and forth along the chain. *You think I don't know how to look after myself? Not like you, I was born in this crazy place. You who come from some island where there are probably palm trees and bananas, you think you know what cold is? On the day I was born, sixty, seventy, maybe eighty years before you, who can tell with you people, the sod walls were completely iced in, five, ten, twenty feet of snow and the midwife couldn't come and there wasn't enough kindling and I was so small and feeble, like a runt pup, and so Mamo and Papo and Johnny all got close on the bed and tried to keep me warm without suffocating me right there.* "Oi, you were shrivelled like a prune as if from the cold," Mamo said, "but the Virgin looked down on us."

When you sigh, still fidgeting and not going away, I want to throw something. *How long has it been since I've wanted to throw something? You think this is hard work,* I want to say, following old people around? *I've scrubbed toilets for a family with seven children, five nearly fully grown and still living in their parents' house, I've stood sorting eggs, who can count how many, until the cold seeped into my joints and I never moved the same again, but you have not known work until you've farmed the prairie from nothing, with nothing but your bare hands. All my childhood I was stooped over. What do you know about such things?*

You shrug, like maybe you've heard what I'm thinking.

"You need something, you let me know then."

As soon as you're gone, the anger dies away, just like that. I hated the work, hated all of it, in the fields, in the houses, in the factories. Who am I to begrudge little brown you who cuts my toenails with such care?

I reach into my pocket for a peppermint, and wait for the words to come back. At first, there's only a siren somewhere and my own sucking noise and the whir, whir, whir. It's so hot outside, but *whir, whir, whir,* always *whir, whir, whir,* and it's cool in here—almost too cool.

Never got found, never got found, never got found.

This time, I'm back on the farm, clearing the roots and the rocks, cleaning the ashes from the oven, spreading hay over the shit.

I'm standing with my underwear and hairbrush and some sauerkraut buns wrapped in a kerchief. I'm not thinking about being on the noisy train for the first time. I'm not thinking about the big city with the strange Indian name. I'm not thinking about missing this place where the Indians laugh at you while you stoop, laugh as they go by on their brown-and-white-spotted horses, with their funny boots and blankets and babies tied to their backs.

I'm thinking about what I've heard, that some hired girls in the city have their own room, with a bed, and a cupboard, and even a lamp.

Papo is outside, stooping to dig or pull or skin something. Mamo is acting funny, walking back and forth across the new wooden floor, like she doesn't trust it yet and needs to keep trying it out. It's hot and sticky outside, not even a breeze, and the room is filled with steam and the bubble of boiling tomatoes.

"You work hard," Mamo says. "You work hard, Tatia. You work hard and I'm sure Christ will reward you."

I can smell the buns in my bundle and want to eat one now, but they're for later. "Yes, Mamo."

Then Mamo stops and grabs a jar of stewed tomatoes from the table. "You take this, for later."

I take the jar and hold it out in front of me. Mamo is acting funny and I don't know what to do with the tomatoes, so I put them back. "It might break."

Mamo turns away and gets her Bible, in the corner by the icons where it always is, and holds it in her hands. "Fine," she says. Then she puts the Bible back and starts stirring over the pots. "You do as you like. You're old now."

"The jar," I say. "It could break on the train."

But she doesn't turn around and I'm already walking, Johnny and Lasia and Terry and Tanya already stopped waving, when she comes from behind, wiping her sweaty face with her apron. "You take this."

It's the tiny crucifix that she wears around her neck, the one all her babies pull at and get slapped over. She's looking at the ground, and the sweat is dripping off her chin, and I think she might be crying, but Mamo never cries.

Three different times, three different baby boys, she'd said to Papo, with no tears. "The Blessed Virgin accepted her son's death, and you, Petro, must accept your son is with Him."

"Be good, Tatia," sweaty Mamo says. "Christ be with you."

I walk away to the station, until my heels feel as if they're being stuck with pins, until I am as sweaty as Mamo, until there's nothing left but road and the words sounding in my head.

Never got found, never got found, never got found.

These were the first. Like a nagging song that stays in your head, the words would repeat over and over and over again, steady and relentless. I used to know what these first ones meant, but am no longer sure. It's the same as earlier, outside, I can remember the crying, but that's all.

"He was crying," I told you.

But you just stuck my feet in the basin, turned up the television. "You just worry about yourself," you said. "You get up on your own, you can fall down. Your grandchildren come here to see how you're doing and what we tell them?"

I've marched these streets, I wanted to say. *I knew these streets before the businesses closed and the hoodlums took over. One great-granddaughter calls it "the core area" with her nose turned up, but I know these streets better than anyone.*

But it may be a lie. When the younger ones come, the great-grandchildren, they look familiar but I can't get at their names. I know there are a few great-greats, probably still in diapers, because they wear them until they are walking and talking these days. All of them, they blur together like the bottom rows of an

It's Me, Tatia

eye chart. I look out the window and it's the same, familiar, but so different that I look away.

I don't care, I wanted to say. *Those grandchildren know no more than you do.*

Now, you with your fidgety little hands wouldn't believe the words that are coming to me, coming from so far away and yet closer than ever. It seems I only have to sit in this olive green chair in the middle of the night and listen.

140 Montrose, 140 Montrose, 140 Montrose.

I'm carefully ironing Mrs. Sullivan's tea towels, white with little mauve flowers, folding first in halves, then in quarters. I'm shaking the feather pillows into pale yellow cases, careful not to catch the silk with my rough skin. I'm walking to mass in my new muskrat coat, flushed hot from the long trolley ride across town.

After Montrose Street, everything here on these streets seems ugly and worn, the people, the sidewalks, the houses. It smells, and I'm starting to smell too, just being here in the muskrat. Since when is it so warm in February?

140 Montrose, 140 Montrose, 140 Montrose.

I step around the melting piles of dog shit, there's no escaping the shit, going as fast as I can, sure to be late, and then *smack*, there's nothing but pain behind my ear.

A voice shouts from behind and I turn. How long has it been since I've heard my language? How long since I've sent any money back home?

"You, what's your name? A man is stepping right in the puddles, splashing his pant legs as he goes. "You, your name."

"Tatia," I start to say, but then remember. "Tilly."

When he stops, he is close enough to touch and breathing

hard. He's wearing a light shirt, open at the neck. "Well, Tatia-Tilly, let me tell you, you look like a bourgeois in that thing. That's why they threw the snowball." He clears his throat, spits into the slush. "Still, they shouldn't have thrown it. Eh?"

He's speaking my language, but I don't really understand.

"Tell me, Tatia. Do you live around here?"

Even though I'm hot, I turn up the collar of my coat. I speak in English.

"I live with the Sullivans at 140 Montrose Street."

"Ah," he says. "A domestic. They couldn't pronounce Tatia?"

I don't know what to say. How would he know such a thing?

"You must be on your way to church, Tatia," he says, as if he can read my mind. "That church, it's always the same, stand up, sit down, sit down, stand up. Eh?"

I feel I should be angry, but there is something about him, stamping his wet feet to keep warm, that makes me smile. He is like no man I have ever seen. Nothing like Papo, nothing like Mr. Sullivan.

"We're having a meeting over there," he says.

He puts his hand under my elbow, clutches at the fur, and I don't stop him.

I know I am going to hell, and yet I let him lead me away. "I'm Saul," he says. "Come."

Saul Solemen. Saul Solemen. Saul Solemen.

I'm polishing Mr. Sullivan's shoes as fast as I can, the sweet-smelling polish flying *swish-swash, swish-swash* over the leather. I'm washing the floor in what they call the "foyer," *ring and swoosh, ring and swoosh,* quick over white tile, then black, white tile, then black. I'm rocking to and fro on the trolley, the red book hugged to my chest so everyone can see, all the way to the deli where Saul is looking at me with his chin in his hands, thin

It's Me, Tatia

hands covered with fine, curly black hair. When he talks, the cigarette bounces on his lip.

"I thought it was so cold that you might not come. But I forgot you have your bourgeois coat, Tatia. Warm February, cold March. What a place, eh?"

He keeps staring, his head in his hands, and I nod. I feel my face flushing and think of my sweaty mamo standing over boiling tomatoes.

He takes the cigarette from his lips and points at me. "But you, Tatia, you don't look like a bourgeois. You have an open and honest face."

No one has ever said such a thing about my face before. What do you do when you can't stop smiling? I put my hand over my mouth.

"And a nice mouth," he says. Then he takes the book and opens it to the marker. "Ah, our hero is in trouble."

I want to grab the book back. It's so good when he explains it, about bringing the power back to the working people so that no one will ever be owned again, not by man and not by religion. It's like the sound of his voice, sure and even, makes me forget that my calluses are bleeding and I've sent no money home for months.

But the reading was hard and I haven't gotten very far. Underneath my sweet, crisp sheets, I fall asleep with the little lamp still on.

"Any questions, Tatia?" he asks.

I think hard for one, want to make sure he knows how hard I've tried.

"Salt of the earth," I say. "The book says salt of the earth and it sounds silly to say the earth is made of salt. What do they mean?"

He takes my hands, so big and chapped, and brushes once, twice with his thumb.

"It means you," he says. He stumps out his cigarette until it's no bigger than a pencil eraser. "You deserve a real worker's position, not cleaning up after some overpaid bureaucrat. I'll talk to some people, don't worry."

I don't really understand, but I don't care. He goes to light another cigarette, and I can still feel his hands, thin hands covered with fine, curly black hair.

Salt of the Earth. Salt of the Earth. Salt of the Earth.

I'm cutting brown packing paper at the plant. Swipe goes the knife…*salt of the earth* goes my head…swipe goes the knife…*salt of the earth* goes my head.

I'm walking home with Saul and Tereza from the meeting and she is making fun of our shift boss, Mr. Rudy.

"C-c-c-come on, girls," she says, "you, you, you j-j-just went t-t-to the, the bathroom."

Even though it's night, it's warm enough to go without a jacket and Saul keeps grabbing my shoulders like he wants to dance right there in the street.

Then Tereza is turning for home and Saul's hand is under my elbow and we're in the back lane behind the bakery. My back is against the brick wall and he is so close I can hear the whistle from his nostrils.

"How long, Tatia," he says, "how long have we known each other? Eh?"

I try to see his face, but it's too dark and he is only a warm, whistling shadow.

"I think four months maybe," he says. "And now we're friends, no?"

All I want is to put my fingers in his curls. Would they feel soft and springy or thick and wiry? I reach up and then I can feel his soft curls in my hand, and taste the sour tobacco on his tongue, and somewhere far away, there is the sound of the street.

He suddenly steps away and grabs my shoulders like when we were walking.

"This," he says, "this, Tatia, is what it's all for. You see? Me a Jew and you a peasant, and all the horrific past of greed and hatred, it will be history. It will be nothing but justice."

I touch his hair again and then he is so close I can feel the buttons of his shirt and the heat of his hands and his legs and his breath, so warm compared to the cool, hard bricks.

Me a Jew. Me a Jew. Me a Jew.

Swipe goes the knife...*me a Jew,* goes my head...swipe goes the knife...*me a Jew*, goes my head.

I'm standing in the toilet stall, holding up my skirt.

"T-t-t-times up," Mr. Rudy shouts.

I don't say anything, just stand there holding my skirt, remembering my papo.

"The Romanians are bastards and the Jews are bootlickers," he said. "They're smart, the Jews, they know who butters their bread and they only screw you 'cause you're a stinkin' Ukrainian, my friend," while Mamo mumbled prayers under her breath.

I run my hands over my stomach and my chest, like Saul did. I think of the spit flying from Papo's mouth, and then the tickling of Saul's tongue, and I punch the wooden door of the stall with all my strength. The latch breaks and hangs like it's dead.

I think of my mamo and papo with no letter for months. I think of leaving the Sullivans before the sun is even up, Mamo's precious gift still under the pillow. I think of Saul, who is a Jew, and who put his tongue in my mouth.

When Mr. Rudy calls again, I say I'm having female troubles and walk out the door.

Someone touches my shoulder and I jump.

When I open my eyes it's too bright and I have to close them again. How did I get into the olive green chair?

I can tell from your strange fishy smell that it's you.

"You want your breakfast here, or downstairs?"

You know I have no appetite, but still you bring it, the runny eggs and dry brown toast, the weak tea and apple juice. You put the tray down on the round table beside me and wait.

I turn away, and you cross your arms like you always do when I don't want your food.

"How you going to feel better if you don't eat? Huh? You going to live on peppermints? Is that how you got be so old? Living on the peppermints?"

You're smiling now, but I don't care. What was it that upset you last night? Someone was crying. I told you someone was crying. A boy. But I might as well be talking to a tractor. For months I told you about the dog I watched through the window, the hungry black one chasing cars and making a nuisance of himself. For months, you waved me away, as if I was talking about dancing leprechauns.

I take the tea from the tray but my hands aren't just stiff, as they usually are. They're shaky like yours were last night, and you have to mop up my housecoat with a paper napkin.

"You want the TV? There's some repeats on the cable. You like them."

You turn the chair so I can see, and more tea spills, but I don't say anything. On the screen a judge is talking to a young man who looks guilty. The lawyer, a young woman, is walking back and forth in a short skirt.

I know these are my shows, the ones where they tell a whole story in one hour. The courtroom drama queen, one of the young ones calls me. But now, the bright screen hurts my eyes and the teacup is unsteady in my hands.

I wasn't done when you came in. What was I doing? What

It's Me, Tatia

did I do before I was the courtroom drama queen? There was a time, I know, before the babies came and the endless eggs and the baby's babies when there were no words in my head at all, when there was nothing to do but sit.

I close my eyes and try hard to remember. The words from the TV blend together like the great-grandchildren, familiar and forgettable.

I'm standing in the park in the warm rain. Saul is at the front somewhere where I can't see him. There is nothing but a sea of shoulders, shiny and wet, so close around me I can hardly breathe.

"They shall not build, and another inhabit," a voice says from far away. "They shall not plant and another eat. For as the days of a tree are the days of my people, and mine elect shall long enjoy the work of their hands."

The words wash over me like the rain, clear and warm. Then there is nothing but a blast of fists in the air, and the shoulders begin to shout, almost all together. It's nothing like the voices at mass, tired and sniffly. It's a giant wave of sound, terrible and wonderful, and when I touch my face, I don't know if I feel rain or tears.

For the first time in my life, I'm doing nothing but sitting. We're on general strike, all of us, the telephone operators and the policemen and the stonemasons, the whole city and me, and I'm wasting time placing a red seven on a black eight. I'm counting the cards, one-two-three, one-two-three, searching for the ones that I need until there's no choice left but to shuffle the cards and start again and again and again.

I'm sitting out on the fire escape in my slip, waiting for the breeze, but all it brings is dirty diapers and other people's greasy supper. Why am I so tired? For ten hours I slept and still didn't want to get out of bed. It's as if my body weighs one thousand pounds.

I'm shuffling the cards, trying not to think of how many days it's been since he's come, how many days with no money, counting the cards, *one-two-three*, putting ace of hearts up top, when I hear someone at the door.

I climb through the window and he hands me a jar of crabapple jelly. His white shirt is stained dark around the collar and his fingernails are black with ink.

The jelly makes me hungry. "There's no buns left," I say.

He takes the cigarette from his mouth and throws it across the floor. "No buns, Tatia? There's going to be arrests. That's what they're saying, there's going to be arrests."

I can't believe this, as if I'm still asleep and dreaming.

He makes a gurgling sound, puts his hands together as if he's begging for spare change. "The strike is over, Tatia. When the powerful are bastards and the weak are buffoons, what can you do?"

There's small bubbles of spit in the corners of his mouth. "Eh, Tatia, can you tell me? I bet you can't."

I can feel my blouse wet beneath the armpits. Who is this Saul with black fingernails and bubbles of spit? I walk over to the smouldering cigarette and stomp it with my bare foot.

But he's looking somewhere else, somewhere out the window and far away.

Look at me! I want to scream. *Tell me that it doesn't have to be this way!*

What do you do when you don't understand?

I kneel down and take his hands. I put them against my chest. "It's me, Tatia," I say.

He makes the gurgling sound again and then is on his knees.

"Tatia, you are so good," he says.

Suddenly the slip is at my waist and there's a sharpness that I don't understand. How could it be with his pants still on? But it's his finger, moving in and out of me while he whispers into my hair, over and over.

He picks me up under the arms and I lie back on the cot

with the bruising springs. I close my eyes and feel the movement again, but this time the pain is worse. No worse, I think, than slamming your finger in a door or spilling boiling water.

Then his tongue is tickling my neck, my cheek, my ear, while he whispers and I'm not thinking of anything. There's only the pain and his tongue and the whispers, so good, so good, and it's all so close and so awful and so good that I can hardly stand it.

When he pushes hard, drops his chest down onto mine, I don't want it to stop.

Please, I want to say. I don't want it to stop, so awful and so good, not for the Jews or for the Ukrainians, or for justice.

He laughs at how I'm trembling. He covers me with a blanket, then his clothes, then mine. He puts all his weight on top of me, and still I tremble.

You take the teacup from my unsteady hand, but I don't want it to be a teacup. I want it to be crabapple jelly. He took it from me as he knelt and let it roll noisily across the floor.

"You not talking to me today? You not watching your shows?"

Not now, I want to say. Please. This is too important.

I want to know what happened to him. I am Tilly, a hard-working stonemason's wife for fifty years, but what about him? I was sleeping and then he was gone.

My chest feels heavy, like he's still lying on top of me. I put a peppermint on my tongue but it doesn't help. Every breath comes long and hard.

You, I want to say, standing there playing with the cross around your neck, you wouldn't understand. It's not good to be old and to never have believed enough.

I could never believe enough in the Virgin, never believe enough in justice.

My young ones have moved far away from here, have foyers of their own, but no matter what, no matter how long I'm on this earth, I know these streets here still smell like the poor. I know you wear my mamo's cross but you still smell strange and fishy and I can't pronounce your name.

I know those shows on the television, with beginning, middle, and end, they're not real.

I know I will never know what happened to him. I didn't care to ask where he lived, as long as he came to me.

"You don't eat, you don't talk, you don't watch the TV. You going to at least have a bath? Huh? A nice bath?"

"A boy was crying," I say. "Outside. When I was outside."

You walk away, shout above the rush of water in the tub. "Why you keep on about that? You don't worry about that. They said a nice policeman help him. What he doing out that late? That's what I want to know. Why they let their kids wander out so late?"

I remember it's the Indians who live here now. It was an Indian boy who was crying, maybe six years old, hugging himself in his T-shirt. He was standing near the glass doors that open onto the dark lane. The doors slid open, just like that, the overhead light popped on, and the boy appeared at the mouth of the lane, crying.

"I don't know which way," he shouted. The snot was running into his mouth. "I got the cherry ones but I don't know which way now."

When I stepped out, the steamy air was like a blanket and I almost fell down in surprise. How long had it been since the air wrapped around me like that? With his blue-black hair, he almost disappeared into the dark. "What's your name?" I asked.

But he wasn't listening. "I don't know which way," he shouted.

Then your little brown hands were pulling me back, back into the safe and cold room, but you didn't know that the words were already there.

Never got found, never got found, never got found.

It's Me, Tatia

I'm walking in snow so deep that it's filling my boots. I can feel the cold metal of the shovel and the lantern through my mittens, and the cow and the oxen are somewhere behind me, making low noises in the dark. I hate this, oh how I hate it, but Mamo is coughing and Johnny is coughing, and the others are too little.

Though I want to be done, I stop because the snow in my boots is melting against my legs. There are lots and lots of stars, but no fireflies. There are fireflies only in the summer, but why is that? Why can't they be there in the winter too, when it's so dark and you have to go out so early and your legs sting so bad?

Never got found, never got found, never got found.

I'm walking again through the deep snow, thinking of Papo's story.

"You remember this," he would say, "you remember the little one, little Mary from not far from here. It was spring planting, and this is true, because I worked the lines with her step-uncle and he wasn't a liar. She left her work and went off to pick some wildflowers and at sundown, her people couldn't find her. Three days go by and all they find is an Indian camp somewhere close and then some people start seeing a bunch of them with a little white girl, but they never got found."

Then Papo would get the big jar from behind the flour sack and pour some into a cup. He'd drink it in one big gulp and his face would turn bright red.

You could feel the heat just standing next to him.

"You see," he'd say. "You work hard or the Indians, they'll snatch you away and you'll go to live in the teepees."

I hang the lantern on a wooden post. Then I hold the shovel far out in front of me and bring it down with all my might.

Crack goes the ice…*never got found,* goes my head…crack goes the ice…*never got found,* goes my head…slush goes the ice…*never got found,* goes my head.

There is a small hole, with black water inside. I step back, one, two, three, and then there is nothing but the sound of the animals, lapping and grunting.

They could still come, I think. I'm alone, and they could come. They could come and steal me away to live in the forest, to wander with pots and babies on my back, to sit high on a horse and laugh at nothing.

The animals are finished drinking, but I stay put. I am lost, lost, lost, but I'm not afraid.

"I can't feel my legs," I say.

But I must've said it out loud because now you're over me, poking at me, upset again.

"You all right? You breathing all right? I can call an ambulance. We go back to the hospital."

Leave me be! I want to shout, like the boy had shouted. Leave me be! Don't ruin it!

I'm with the wild Indians, who have swept me up into the tall poplars to laugh at nothing. I'm with curly-haired Saul, who whispers "so good" and makes me bleed until my bulky body falls away and there's nothing but that feeling so deep inside, painful and fine. I'm lost, lost, lost, where there is no Tatia, or Tilly, or stupid cows that need a drink.

But you poke and fidget, poke and fidget. You look at me like my young ones do, trying to understand what I don't understand myself.

I didn't mean to upset you.

"No," I say. "I'm fine. I want a bath."

You run to turn off the water, and then your small hands are on me. They're small, those hands, but when you help me up, I'm always surprised by their strength.

"You sure you ready?"

Yes.

SOURCES

What follows is a list of sources for the "facts" preceeding the stories in this collection. On-line entries as of March 25, 2014.

Black Bear Facts

Landriault, L.J., Obbard, M.E., and Rettie, W.J. "Nuisance Black Bears and What to Do with Them." OMNR, Northeast Science & Technology. TN-042. 2000. 20p. Web. 6 Aug. 2014. <http://www.stcharlesontario.ca/upload/documents/neusance-bear.pdf>.

Origin of "Manitoba"

"The Origin of the Name Manitoba." Government of Manitoba. Web. 6 Aug. 2014. <www.gov.mb.ca/chc/louis_riel/pdf/origin_mb_name.pdf>.

Swampy Cree Creation Legend

Scott, Simeon, and Xavier Sutherland. "Legends and Narratives: Swampy Cree." 1-39. NLIP Institute, 2006. Web. 6 Aug. 2014. <imp.lss.wisc.edu/~jrvalent/old_nlip/NLIP_Institute_2006_bu/attachments/ellis_cree_stories_intro.pdf>.

Scott, Simeon. "Where the First People Came From." *Spider Language.* St. Norbert Arts Centre. Web. 6 Aug. 2014. <snac.mb.ca/projects/spiderlanguage/firstpeople.html>.

Scott, Simeon. "Where the First People Came From." 2009. *Doug Ellis Audio Collection.* Spoken Cree, C. Douglas Ellis. 2012. Web. 6 Aug. 2014. <www.spokencree.org/Stories/browseby/dialects>.

Facts about Ukraine and Ukrainians

"Ukrainian Canadian." Wikipedia. 14 June 2014. Web. 6 Aug. 2014. <en.wikipedia.org/wiki/Ukrainian_Canadian>.

Oleksandr, Kramar. "We Were 52 Million: Where Did 6 Million Ukrainians Go?" 14 Mar. 2012. The Ukrainian Week: International Edition. Web. 6 Aug. 2014. <ukrainianweek.com/Society/43071>.

Origin of "You Can Call Me Al"
"You Can Call Me Al." Wikipedia. 3 July 2014. Web. 6 Aug. 2014. <en.wikipedia.org/wiki/You_Can_Call_Me_Al>.

Chernobyl Death Toll
"Effects of the Chernobyl Disaster." Wikipedia. 16 July 2014. Web. 6 Aug. 2014. <en.wikipedia.org/wiki/Effects_of_the_Chernobyl_disaster>.

First Icelanders in Canada
"Icelandic Canadian." Wikipedia. 26 May 2014. Web. 6 Aug. 2014. <en.wikipedia.org/wiki/Icelandic_Canadian>.

Belugas
"Beluga Whale." Wikipedia. 29 July 2014. Web. 6 Aug. 2014. <en.wikipedia.org/wiki/Beluga_whale>.

Elf School
"About the Elfschool." The Elfschool. Web. 6 Aug. 2014. <www.elfmuseum.com>.

Icelanders at the Movies
"10 Surprising Facts about Iceland." Kizaz. 2013. Web. 6 Aug. 2014. <kizaz.com/2013/12/20/10-surprising-facts-about-iceland/>.

Churchill Climate
"Churchill, Manitoba." Wikipedia. 6 Aug. 2014. Web. 6 Aug. 2014. <en.wikipedia.org/wiki/Churchill,_Manitoba>.

The Metis
"Métis people (Canada)." Wikipedia. 8 July 2014. Web. 6 Aug. 2014. <en.wikipedia.org/wiki/Métis_people_(Canada)>.

Sources

Autism

Mandal, Ananya . "Autism History." *News Medical.* AzoMedical. 2014. Web. 6 Aug. 2014. <www.news-medical.net/health/Autism-History.aspx>.

Temple Grandin's Hug Box

"Temple Grandin." Wikipedia. 30 July 2014. Web. 6 Aug. 2014. <en.wikipedia.org/wiki/Temple_Grandin>.

Louis Riel's Last Words

"Final Trial Statement & Subsequent Renounciation of Louis Riel." 1885. *Famous Trials.* Douglas O. Linder, UMKC School of Law, 2014. Web. 6 Aug. 2014. <law2.umkc.edu/faculty/projects/ftrials/riel/rieltrialstatement.html>.

India

"61 Interesting Facts about India." *Random Facts.* Random History. 2014. Web. 6 Aug. 2014. <facts.randomhistory.com/2009/07/21_india.html>.

The Roma

Fonesca, Isabel. *Bury Me Standing: The Gypsies and Their Journey.* New York: Random House, 1995. Print. 322.

"Romani People." Wikipedia. 5 Aug. 2014. Web. 6 Aug. 2014. <en.wikipedia.org/wiki/Romani_people>.

"Roma Culture: An Introduction." *Factsheets on Roma.* Romani Projekt, Council of Europe. Web. 6 Aug. 2014. <romafacts.uni-graz.at/index.php/culture/introduction/roma-culture-an-introduction>.

Muhammad's Hair Colour

Earlson, Karl. "Nordic Arabs." *Karl Earlson's Racial History Research Page.* Web. 6 Aug. 2014. <marchofthetitans.com/earlson/nordicarabs.htm>.

Persia

"History of Iran." Wikipedia. 3 Aug. 2014. Web. 6 Aug. 2014. <en.wikipedia.org/wiki/History_of_Iran>.

"Paradise." Wikipedia. 3 Aug. 2014. Web. 6 Aug. 2014. <en.wikipedia.org/wiki/Paradise>.

Iranian-Canadian Beauties
"Iranian Canadian." Wikipedia. 25 June 2014. Web. 6 Aug. 2014. <en.wikipedia.org/wiki/Iranian_Canadian>.

Sperm Bank
Barton, Adriana. "No Redheads Allowed: Sperm Bank Rejects 'Ginger' Donors." The Globe and Mail. 19 Sept. 2011. Web. 6 Aug. 2014. <http://www.theglobeandmail.com/life/the-hot-button/no-redheads-allowed-sperm-bank-rejects-ginger-donors/article617528/>.

China
"World Population. Wikipedia. 4 Aug. 2014. Web. 6 Aug. 2014. <en.wikipedia.org/wiki/World_population>.

"Toilet Paper." Wikipedia. 17 July 2014. Web. 6 Aug. 2014. <en.wikipedia.org/wiki/Toilet_paper>.

"Three Gorges Dam." Wikipedia. 30 July 2014. Web. 6 Aug. 2014. <en.wikipedia.org/wiki/Three_Gorges_Dam>.

"One-Child Policy." Wikipedia. 31 July 2014. Web. 6 Aug. 2014. <en.wikipedia.org/wiki/One-child_policy>.

Bramen, Lisa. "The History of Chopsticks." *Smithsonian Magazine*. 5 Aug. 2009. Web. 6 Aug. 2014. <www.smithsonianmag.com/arts-culture/the-history-of-chopsticks-64935342/?no-ist>.

The Winnipeg General Strike
Masters, D.C. *The Winnipeg General Strike*. Toronto: University of Toronto Press, 1973. Print. 159.

Reilly, J. Nolan. "Winnipeg General Strike." 2 July 2006. *The Canadian Encyclopedia*. Web. 6 Aug. 2014. <www.thecanadianencyclopedia.com/en/article/winnipeg-general-strike/>.

Sources

"First Teachers Trained on Winnipeg General Strike in MFL Supported Manitoba Museum Project." 19 Mar. 2013. Manitoba Federation of Labour. Web. 6 Aug. 2014. <mfl.ca/first-teachers-trained-winnipeg-general-strike-mfl-supported-manitoba-museum-project>.

"Lesson 1: Creating a Newspaper." *High School Resources.* 2001. CBC Learning. Web. 6 Aug. 2014. <www.cbc.ca/history/LESSONS-SE4EP12CH2PA1LE.html>.

Residential School History

"Canadian Indian Residential School System." Wikipedia. 6 Aug. 2014. Web. 6 Aug. 2014. <en.wikipedia.org/wiki/Canadian_Indian_residential_school_system>.

"Residential Schools." *Truth and Reconciliation Commission of Canada.* Web. 6 Aug. 2014. <www.trc.ca/websites/trcinstitution/index.php?p=4>.

"History & Background." *Reconciliation Canada.* Web. 6 Aug. 2014. <reconciliationcanada.ca/welcome/history/>.

Acknowledgements

Much thanks to my editor, Wayne Tefs, who challenged me to create a book worthy of tough-ass Winnipeggers and to my husband, Duncan Thornton, who sometimes wishes he lived in London but remains a stoic prairie boy at heart.

"It's Me, Tatia" was first published in the anthology *Kobzar's Children* (Fitzhenry and Whiteside, 2006).

"Boy Lost in Wild" was first published in *The Malahat Review* (Winter 2001).

"You Can Call Me Al" was first published in the anthology *Up All Night* (Thistledown Press, 2001).

This book was written with the generous support of the Canada Council for the Arts and the Manitoba Arts Council.